I0626124

Kept

JIM ARNOLD

Copyright © 2016 Jim Arnold
All rights reserved.
Published by Eureka Street Press

ISBN: 0996938001
ISBN 13: 9780996938006

Connor Hurst always wondered if George turned out the way he did because of his mother.

Alma Gomez and that shiny, long black hair: George always said it was scented with Mexican fragrance, a type of sage. The name of it was *salvia*.

Connor's cock heavier now at the notion of salvia, which grew in a valley near San Ignacio on the road from Guadalajara to the sea, because George's hair smelled the same as hers and the scent was now deep in the skin, too. It is wet—Connor's cock, that is—straining against the slim-cut gray trousers necessary this cool evening at Sydney Harbour.

Connor's nose in George's hair, deep in. Salvia. He reaches down to his ankle, scratching the itch under the stained compression bandage, another lingering reminder of the unfortunate tram "accident."

A bottle of Tooheys New beer sits on a black tray. The napkin, navy blue to match the label, flutters in the easy night breeze. It takes all he's got not to pitch it into the sea.

Connor never met Alma Gomez, not really, but he heard the voice. Inside her trailer, or around in back, not ever really sure from his driver's seat just where she was. Saw the back of her head—maybe shiny, long black hair. The crappy Gomez trailer out in Mecca, California, its cheap siding peeled, the relentless desert sun slowly but completely destroying it, turning it back to sand.

Inside were the other Gomez boys, George's brothers, the young ones. George told him the names—but he would forget, though that was a lie (they were Chuy and Jesse)—as he turned to you with that smile, those glow-in-the dark teeth he had.

"Here are my beloved brothers," he said, so serious, out there in Mecca, with mama, stuck on this patch of cursed dirt! "There's no future, *papi*, no life for them unless I make one for them," he'd say, making Connor laugh: "I make it for them. "

Connor knew her name was Alma Gomez, not much more than that. Alma, their word for *soul*. He knew there were bad souls as well as good souls and that enormous group somewhere in between.

It's possible Alma Gomez put that shade into her eldest son, his Jorge, his George, made him turn out the way he did. After all, his father was long gone. That's what he said, anyway. Maybe *that* was a lie, too.

Alma knew where her old man was: close by, in spirit anyway. The one time Connor asked, George dismissed him as a common field hand who couldn't even read road signs.

That was a lie, too, Connor thinks, looking down at his feet, covered in those nice brown-on-brown Cucinelli wingtips; nice shoes the handsome thirty-two-year-old lifted from the back of the duty-free store in Honolulu while a clerk chatted up a rich Chinese matron.

A sip of the beer, before looking, just one more time, in the bag, and counting, *again*, the money that nowhere near added up to what it should be!

What it should be, needs to be, is double or triple or quadruple what's there. Connor used to see red, and shake, then erupt. But he's a bit older and a bit calmer now and instead he sees Jorge Sr. and Alma Gomez's bleached teeth flash as they fight over trendy marble counter selections at Harrigan's Home Remodel in Palm Desert.

He sees his George, his Jorge, counting out the cash for a year-old Mercedes C-Class sedan (black, of course) at Brand Boulevard of Cars in Glendale, California.

He sees skinny Chuy and Jesse locking their new all-terrain mountain bikes at La Quinta Country Club on their way to golf lessons.

Golf! He trembles and his eyes fill. *He played you, Connor Hurst.*

The Tooheys New and the tray it is on fly into Sydney Harbour.

If George were in front of him right now he'd be a fucking dead man.

1

It took Jorge Gomez five minutes to try on all four T-shirts and two tank tops. These items in the black plastic crate next to his narrow single mattress and box spring were the extent of his above-the-waist wardrobe. *Makes it easy and quick,* he thought. *Verano o invierno,* he knew what to wear. He favored bright colors, the greens or maybe a piercing orange that would show off his smooth dark skin and black hair. His people weren't the type to draw attention that way, but he would change that.

Easy and quick.

All the shirts were from Angel Wing Thrift Store in Palm Springs. He would change that, too. One had a small hole in the front down near the bottom hem. It was his favorite, somebody's donated Abercrombie & Fitch, pale blue. He loved the way it hugged his shoulders and his small but well-formed pecs. He loved the way boys sometimes put a finger into that hole to touch his tight stomach down there. He wouldn't let Mama fix this one. He'd wear it today.

He turned to look at his five-foot-six frame in the dusty mirror tacked up between his little brothers' bunk beds. *Not bad, you sexy gay American man,* he thought, even though the top bunk cut off his head. He'd wear his tightest jeans, the Wranglers, though it was sure to be 110 degrees. He thought his legs too skinny for shorts; he didn't want to look like anybody's little boy.

He reached between his legs, pulling the underside of the *cojones* forward so there appeared more of a bulge. That's what they liked to see; that's what they wanted, *creo que sí*, those beautiful, sometimes rich white men in Palm Springs.

All the walking in the hot, awful east valley around Mecca, California, made him lean, sometimes so much his pants would slide off his hips. Not in a dangerous, sexy way, showing a little bit of the damp, curly dark hairs but more like in a "too dirt-poor to afford anything else" kind of way.

He bent forward a bit, so he could see his face, cocked a black eyebrow and tried out a look. Truth was he couldn't ever get himself a proper pair of pants or a proper car that was acceptable in the daylight without a little bit of help.

This trip would fix that.

When Alma Gomez was mad she strode down that trailer hallway and her movable house shook. Yet she was not a big woman. Through the flimsy pressed-wood wall, yellowing with filmy decay, Jorge imagined her expression. A frown, most certainly. She shook her head and by extension that long dark hair (which he inherited), most definitely.

The door bent toward him as she pounded. Twice. *Bang-bang.* She wanted to know what he was doing in there: "Why don't you come out of there?" She yelled, "Your brothers are waiting. Your brothers need to change. That is your brothers' room too; don't forget that, *mijo. You don't own it.*"

You don't own it! Jorge Gomez didn't own much of anything. But two things needed his attention. His fake ID, the one that called him George Gomes, a little twist that instantly made him Anglo and American. Stuff that one in the back pocket. No, wait, the front is better; the white men in Palm Springs don't like it when there's anything in the back to ruin a nice, tight, bubble-ass view.

And the other thing, that magazine: Jorge forgot what it was called because the cover got lost somewhere sometime in the past. It was the only porno he had and not even something purchased, but something found in a house they cleaned after somebody moved, in the pile of old paint cans and rags and cheap vodka bottles and ripped-up sky-blue swimming pool floats from China. This magazine with its naked erect men called out to him like a car alarm.

He lifted the single mattress and shoved the beautiful men far under it, way back, almost to the wall on top of the box spring, *seguro* so far back his brothers would never find it.

There was Alma Gomez banging on the door again. Just about ready to open up, but he needed the shades. Jorge didn't like it when his mother looked him in the eye. It spooked him; she could spot the lie a mile away and was always, always searching.

He opened the door. There she was, her fist raised, ready to hit it one more time. He backed up. She sighed and shook her head, the long dark hair flying.

"Your brothers need to get ready for school. What are you doing in there, *mijo?*" She looked him up and down. Chuy and Jesse, miniature versions of himself, exactly what he looked like at age seven or eight, two heads of black hair, gray-white jockey shorts that came up to their navels, standing one on either side of Alma Gomez.

"Your brothers need to *get ready.*"

Jesse and Chuy rushed past him, a good opportunity to adjust the shades with the one scratch, to hide whatever it was in his eyes she could read. The boys weren't curious like he was. Besides, they weren't strong enough to lift the mattress and discover the magazine.

Don't block the door, Mama. Let me out of your ugly trailer! She went on and on and on about Padre H. Sanchez, some job he might have for number one son, Jorge. Though she didn't seem overly excited about the possibilities of this; more of a report to him as promised. Many things Alma Gomez might have been, but at least she was known among the Mecca Mexicans for keeping her word.

Jorge nodded, the appropriate response. He slipped past her, sliding down the tiny hall and out into the dust.

God in his heaven was merciful today. Jorge didn't have to wait long for the bus at the stop outside the Sunny Dreams Two trailer park. If they had jobs, most of the local men were already in the fields down in Brawley or Thermal and, if not, they were waiting to be picked at the Home Depot in Indio or, better yet, inside their trailers, stained shades drawn, a forty popped open, TV tuned to fútbol.

Few cars passed him, and none he recognized. If he stood still, drivers might not even notice him, a small, lean man, barely five-foot-six, standing next to a palm tree next to that uneven, deadly, pink-blossomed oleander hedge that hugged the Sunny Dreams Two slump-stone wall.

Fix the stupid brakes, Jorge whispered as the dirty bus with the "Palm Springs" headsign squealed, lurching toward him to its stop in the sand.

He took the old cassette player, a dusty Walkman he'd found in an unmarked, unsorted bin at the same place he got his shirt, the Angel Wing Thrift Store. It came with the English course cassettes as a bonus package deal, wrapped up in blue masking tape, designed for a Spanish-speaking business traveler encountering the American corporate world back in the 1990s.

He'd practice these phrases in a little whisper, mostly for the pronunciation, which was why Jorge always preferred a window seat. Most days he'd see the reflection of his lips moving in this new language he had miraculously acquired against the magnificent backdrop of Mount San Jacinto. Today was phrase repetition:

"Repeat: Where is the concierge?" the tape said.

"Where is the concierge?" Jorge whispered.

"Repeat: My computer port does not work."

"My computer port does not work."

"Repeat: What time will my laundry be ready?"

"My computer port does not work. It's shit."

■ ■ ■

The Palm Springs bus station stood across the street from Desert Consolidated Savings Bank, out of business now, though its digital temperature sign still worked and it said 113 degrees. Jorge tossed the cassette player into his backpack and fell out of the bus with the rest of the passengers, pausing to turn his cheek up to a hissy but cool air-conditioning vent.

Once he was on the asphalt, the heat hit him with an unstoppable, seeping force that tingled even the tiny hairs deep inside his ears.

Funny how the people on the bus so rapidly dispersed, or maybe not so funny, as there was that imperative to get out of the sun before one fried.

Another person remained in the station lot, and she was under the awning of a vacant building opposite. At least, Jorge thought this person was a she. You could never be sure in Palm Springs! The elderly body in a wheelchair was hidden by a large straw sunhat, draped at an angle as if the owner were taking a nap. Dirty white plastic bags full of possessions hung from the chair's rear push handles.

Of course, only then did a passing cop car also see this and make a lazy U-turn. Jorge knew wheelchair woman would die out here in the heat if left alone for too long, but still the old fear struck, so he lowered his head and looked away, like a dog does when it hopes to be invisible.

■ ■ ■

Desert Sun reporter Nancy Argento liked not answering the always-ringing phone. She'd already turned down the volume once on the desk set, and maybe she should again: *Let's not alienate these resort-town folks more than we already have.*

The petite blonde smiled as she thought about this, looking over her new book's cover, noticing once again how her name was two point sizes bigger than the title, *A Death at Smoketree.*

The work phone was set to go to voice mail after five rings so as not to make her crazy. Nancy was still surprised there were so many calls to a reporter here, in this small town, in this resort city; you'd never guess there'd be anything they might consider "news" here.

She'd arrived a year earlier, freshly fired from the *Cleveland Plain Dealer.* She'd worried there would never be another job for her in journalism, yet here she was, in a cubicle filled with papers and the novel she wrote. *A Death at Smoketree.*

Tall Ted Ligett rested his chin on the top of the partition that separated their newsroom spaces. Which was a little bit creepy, this animated jack-o'-lantern / decapitation horror, like that poor guy from the *Wall Street Journal*. Nancy shuddered; she hated it when Ted did that.

He spent too much time in the sun in a place where the UV Index was most often "extreme." She pressed a hand into her tummy, below the navel, and held it there.

"My friend Nicole stood at the door with one of those hand-counter clicker things, like they do at a club? Seventy-two people showed."

"That's it?" He cocked his head to the left.

Always a challenge, Ted: an inchoate rivalry that made things more interesting. He was old for that surfer-boy haircut, but she hadn't said anything about it. Maybe because she wasn't sure it was *real*. Maybe because she was trying to turn over a new leaf. Be nicer to be around. Avoid getting fired again.

She told him an audience of seventy-two was great at a book reading, actually fantastic because it was summer and most of the ladies who did, in fact, read, were back in Canada floating on a cool lake. Nancy Argento, author, was also scheduled the following week at Blue Collie Pages out in Phoenix. Not that any of it mattered to Ted.

His eyes were locked on her desktop, but it wasn't the great cover of *A Death at Smoketree* he was looking at. It was her digital camera, and not even that; she'd attached an orange-haired troll doll to the strap. He'd think it juvenile, most likely; he'd think it unprofessional. She kept it because it reminded her of a time before worry.

"Hate to bust up our little DIY literary chitchat, but Hart's got an old homeless gal PSPD dropped off in our ever-popular shaded courtyard. Might be a story there," he said.

And what could *that* possibly be, she wondered, though their editor, Hart, must have his reasons. A thousand old women in the valley like this one and it was tragic.

■ ■ ■

Nancy hated the noise her black two-inch heels made as they scraped across the glazed tiles of the ground-floor courtyard the paper shared with what was, essentially, a lifeless mall. Dead, except for the entrepreneurial Laotian lady who wheeled her silver espresso cart in every morning and thus got any business that found its way to the shade in this insane summer heat.

Nancy could wear simple flip-flops to work and totally get away with it. Why she kept up the fancy office dress more appropriate to Ohio than a town where every other city block was a dusty piece of wilderness hiding rattlesnakes was a mystery. The heels made her small frame look bigger, and she could almost fake intimidation; she'd kick them off as soon as she sat down with the old lady.

At least Virginia McCadden didn't smell. She told Nancy to call her Ginny. She needed the California license only for identification purposes, she said; the Lincoln had been sold years ago and she took cabs now. She knew most of them by first name, her Palm Springs cabbies, the nice desert rats who looked out for her.

It was hard to believe this eighty-two-year-old woman had ever driven or had ever owned a *Yugo*, much less a Lincoln.

She wore what looked like a nightgown, white with a blue cornflower pattern, though the white had grayed. Below were ankle-length athletic socks, a darker shade of blue. They were covered with summer dust.

The oversized straw hat was a bit too big to be fashionable, but Ginny McCadden did wear lipstick, a standby Jungle Red, while Nancy preferred the darker, bloodred color she'd admired on those new vampire shows on TV.

Ginny removed the top from the paper coffee cup. "Medicine, to put in?" she whispered.

Within a few minutes Ted Ligett was tableside, having made the "emergency" trip over to Cork 'n' Bottle. He towered over their shaded courtyard table, pouring whiskey into Ginny's cup, the cheap brand obscured by a black plastic bag.

He made a move to pour some liquor into Nancy's coffee as well, but she clamped her hand down over it, throwing him an annoyed squint. Ginny wasted no time, sipping ladylike before telling Nancy she'd been evicted from her *own house. How is that even allowed?* Her light blue eyes bugged out.

"Back up, honey. Tell me what happened to you," Nancy said. Foreclosures happened every day; there were a million stories like this; she must know this.

Especially out here.

Especially this year.

Ted wasn't getting enough attention. He shifted his weight from foot to foot, holding the booze with both hands, making everyone nervous.

"I lived there nineteen years; they come over one day and say I need improvements."

"Who came over? Improvements—what do you mean?"

Ginny raised her cup to Ted. After a glance at Nancy, he poured in a little bit more.

Ginny said it was the "dagos over on Palm Canyon." The dagos said she needed improvements, a new kitchen, a new tub. More.

"Greco? Greco & Greco?" Nancy exchanged a look with Ted.

"They do the fix-up, the house looks great, but I can't pay his note." Ginny explained: "Then the nice man Sy Greco tells me he'll make the payments for me and I just pay him rent, my exact same old amount. But it wasn't the same amount; it was much more."

Ginny pushed her cup to the edge of the table near Ted.

"You know, I'm not the fucking bartender here," he said.

"Ginny, you get more when you finish the story," Nancy said. "But I need to hear every detail. We have plenty of medicine."

Pleading with Ted, she mouthed the word "Stay."

2

Connor Hurst should have washed the truck before rolling it up to the Jones home. A more professional, polished look was what he strove for each and every day, but this morning it was not coming together the way it usually did.

The shitty, dusty, red Greco & Greco logos on the silver truck doors were chipped along their edges. Not a good look for the town's best, if not largest, remodeling outfit, he thought. Better if the company letters were clean and smooth.

On the other hand, Connor looked fine. He looked so Irish he might have been a Celtic warrior or a leering country priest in some other, less ordinary life. He told everybody he was black Irish, though nobody really knew what that meant; even he wasn't sure. He guessed his dark hair, so brown it read black, and the striking blue eyes were evidence enough. His looks had stunned enough women—and men—over the last few years to make further explanation unnecessary.

Connor and his passenger, the skinny boy Jacy Martin, fell out of the pickup into the 115-degree heat of the fresh, late morning asphalt, its chemical odor signaling what Connor liked to think of as a sign of industrial progress: They were making some headway with this house; their actions had consequences.

And they made quite a pair. Dark, Native American and short, squirrely Jacy's role was always sidekick to the regal Connor: the shadow side, Lone Ranger and Tonto.

The younger Jacy wasn't the type to trust too much; he was the type who glanced behind him before talking. But Connor knew it wasn't prudent that Jacy told stories of their tribal chief shooting and killing protected sheep, even if it was on the res, on their own land, in their own fucking *nation*.

That kind of thing got around.

Jacy spat on the red gravel oval at the center of the Joneses' circular drive, just missing a perfectly round blue barrel cactus. Connor ignored this. He'd do the same, but never with anybody around. *I mean, come on.* He figured the Joneses had to be the richest black family in Palm Springs. They had to be. *Look at this place.*

The low, Spanish-style house loomed substantial from the street, but even that was a cheat. It stood at the top of a small rise, then spread out in back, rooms tumbling down to a pool and a fucking tennis court where the landscape leveled off.

As dark as Alice Jones was, Connor wondered if she needed sunscreen at the pool. She told him she never played tennis. Her son had, though, and quite well, so even if he was gone now, the court was good luck and they kept it up.

She opened the finely distressed, heavy oak door with one hand— which, of course, showed off her diamond and gold wedding rings, as well as a big-ass separate emerald on her index finger.

The pounding hammers of the Greco & Greco workers already inside rose, as did Jacy's panting, which reminded Connor of a nervous dog. Then there was Alice Jones, holding the door wide open, wearing one of her green-and-black caftans from Africa. Her tits jiggled. No bra today; she knew he was coming.

Jacy was used to the drill. He entered first after a clipped "Ma'am" to Alice, heading straight for the guys who were finishing up new drywall in the media room, which was next to the library, which was down from the dining room.

Far enough away from Alice's bedroom, which was the only important location.

She clutched Connor by the forearm and led him down the hallway, a gallery where they'd positioned spotlights to hit the artwork at precise sweet spots dictated by a professional curator flown in all the way from New York.

"Mr. Hurst, can you come with me?" she asked. "I've got some problems to show you in the back."

He threw Jacy a smirk, though the smaller man was already out of sight. Small problems in the back—*Yeah, right, Alice, I bet you got a few!*

At the end of the long hallway a door closed, blocking out the daylight—as so many of these desert homes seemed designed to do. Not a bad idea when you had things to hide.

■ ■ ■

Outside, in the brilliant sun, white-haired Bernard Jones inched his way up the Camino del Monte cul-de-sac and saw not one but two Greco & Greco trucks in his driveway, parked on that almost imperceptible incline. So he had to put his car on the street. He didn't like the idea of having to walk the forty or so extra paces to his door. It was hard enough getting out of the low Porsche.

Jacy watched from the media room window, located at the front of the house, a window that would soon be fitted with a custom removable blackout shade for movie nights. But today it was simply an empty window.

This is gonna be some trouble! Just what Connor Hurst has coming to him. White boy gets away with too damn much; about time someone kicked his ass! Jacy chuckled into his fist, a spasm of delight racing up his spine, making him jump.

Though this Bernard Jones was a short old fart. Would they take it out to the pool, or maybe all the way down to that tennis court? No, Mr. Jones wouldn't want to get into it that way. He'd have a gun, probably close at hand. Probably had several—*look at all this art shit in here.* Plus, there weren't many around Palm Springs who looked like the Joneses: When you got some color and you got some money, people don't like it. Jacy knew that well enough from the tribe going from poor red to red with money.

But sometimes loyalty trumps the desire to see someone get his lesson. Or maybe it was pure practicality, having to get along with your co-workers no matter who they were, even if they were Connor Hurst. So Jacy moved into the hallway, a cheerful Indian ready to intercept a rich American nigger.

■ ■ ■

Meantime Connor had Alice up on all fours on her big bed, which was covered with a taut blue-green abstract duvet with contrasting tan-and-black-striped pillows, one of which her head was now buried in.

Her caftan was still partly on, bunched up in folds over her shoulders and her neck, covering her face. Her beautiful cocoa ass pointed up toward the ceiling. Connor had pushed in, leaning over to whisper, "You like 'em young, don'tcha, Alice; you like 'em white, too!"

Her voice was muffled by the pillows. "I like 'em hard," he thought he heard her say. He wasn't exactly sure because there was a commotion, activity unplanned and unwanted, somewhere not too far outside the bedroom door.

Bernard Jones was in the hallway, the hallway gallery, where their important and expensive paintings and sculpture had been positioned by the New York decorator with custom track lighting that had to be redone four times before Alice would approve it.

The heavy, dark wooden door at the end of the hallway, the door to his bedroom, was closed.

Bernard Jones headed toward it.

The short Indian was in the way. "We marked places in the sheetrock where your speakers will go. Let me show you, Mr. Jones," the little man said, positioning himself directly in front of him, blocking his advance, trying to turn him around; then again, not trying too hard. "Let me show you the media room, man."

"Get out of here, you fucking little *bug*! Alice?"

But Connor had already put it together. He was off poor old Alice, grabbing his pants, his Greco & Greco workshirt, his shoes, looking up to the ceiling for an instant, asking if she'd ever considered some "nice regal crown molding," then easing himself behind the lux drapes and out the slider door. But not before Alice tossed him a couple of Benjamins—and his socks.

"Go!" she whispered, blowing him a kiss, already examining herself in the mirror, arranging the caftan back in its correct matronly order.

■ ■ ■

The big dog lies in the partial shade of a mesquite tree that at this time of day still covers its position on the low diving board at Sy and Pilar Greco's pool. Eyes open a mere slit, but still watchful and always, always waiting; its tongue hangs out, a tiny, thin stream of slobber beading down to the pristine aqua of the water below.

Across the pool, Candy's master, Sy, rakes the surface with his skimmer. He is tan and trim, his mint-green Tommy Bahama print shirt unbuttoned halfway down his chest; this task is more meditative than effective. Sy Greco's got Mexicans to do the real cleaning.

A doorbell chimes at the far front of the house, but of course, Candy hears it. The Rottweiler raises her head a fraction of an inch, as she knows this man already; she smelled him seconds ago, before he even rang.

Connor walks onto the patio, purposeful, knowing the landscape well, taking the long way around the pool, thus avoiding the diving board and its occupant. He's got the same Greco & Greco shirt on as before, now neatly tucked into tan summer-weight slacks, no trace of Bernard and Alice Jones's sandy flower beds evident.

"Signatures, boss," he says, tapping an old-style, boxy, dark leather briefcase under his arm.

He sets it down on a glass-covered patio table, the little latches snapping up. Candy's ears pull back just a tiny bit. Sy Greco nods, eyeing the papers inside.

"What's that you've got for me?" he asks.

Connor turns to look around, noting that the only other living thing besides Sy and the cicadas is the black dog on the diving board. Then Sy is there, face-to-face, leaning in, his lips meeting the younger man's.

Tastes like chai, Connor thinks. Like usual.

"Contracts, papers to sign. A Ruth Hardy Park Nyman remodel, the one you had your eye on. It's ours. And oh—a reporter called, Nancy something or other, from the *Desert Sun.*"

Now Sy's arms are around him, pulling him in. Connor tries to remember if he kissed Alice, and was she wearing any perfume today? *Wait, that's not important*—Sy wouldn't mind, or might even like it if Connor smelled a bit like a woman—as long as it wasn't his wife, Pilar Greco.

Across the pool, Candy stretched and padded over to the cooler dirt under the pink oleander. She flopped down in a heap, eyes still on the men across the pool.

Sy inched them both backward till he fell into a padded club chair. He sat down, reeling Connor in by his belt, undoing the buckle, then peeling his slacks off his hips.

Connor locked eyes with Candy. It was weird being watched by a dog, and this wasn't the first time. Still, Sy Greco, even if he was almost sixty, gave the best head ever. As he swallowed him, Connor nodded to the dog, giving her a little conspiratorial wink.

Better blow jobs, even, than Pilar Greco, and hers were pretty damn fine, he thought. *You saw that too, didn't you, little doggie? Good thing you can't talk.*

It's good dogs can't talk.

Sy moaned softly. But there were other noises now, noises that made Connor nervous. A scratch over here, a muffled voice from around a wall.

Sy liked to play on the edge, so it was even possible Pilar was home, sleeping late. Or, in the more likely event she was gone, the maid, that Ukrainian cunt Marina, could step out on the patio at any time for any reason, find them and destroy them.

But she wouldn't do that, since Sy was her boss.

You wouldn't have to worry about this shit all the time if you'd just take it easy. Find one good person; call it a day.

Yet a part of Connor knew such propriety on his part was as likely as Candy ordering Sy's men around in *español*: not going to happen.

He brushed Sy's gray head as he peaked and flowed into the older man's mouth, grateful Sy's strong hands bolstered his thighs, keeping him from falling.

After they finished, it sometimes took forever till Sy would let go. This was one of those times. If Sy had tasted Alice, he didn't let on.

"I need to rinse off," Connor said, removing his Greco & Greco shirt, letting it drop onto the salmon-pink pool decking.

Then he was underwater, the silent world closing in, all traces of both Alice and Sy removed, just like that. Naked, Connor stretched out for as long as he could along the cool blue pool bottom. When he broke the surface of the water a second before his lungs would explode, Candy was there at pool's edge, waiting.

■ ■ ■

Sy had other documents he needed Connor to drop back at the Greco & Greco company office, so he was able to leave the house without making some other excuse. Candy escorted him to the front door, and she seemed to enjoy the parting pat on the head. Maybe they'd bond after all.

That would be good, not only because Candy was a moody Rottweiler, unpredictable, never good to be on the bad side of, but also because it would please Sy Greco no end if his dog liked you.

The sun had fallen over the mountain now. It was a shade cooler, though still over 100. Palm Springs bathed in that rosy predusk light, the way Connor preferred.

Everything had a softer edge, benign, looked hopeful—even those low-slung whitewashed buildings along Indian Canyon slated for urban renewal, a desert slum, if that was even a thing. They'd been built in the 1950s and '60s for retail, car dealerships and warehousing—back when Frank Sinatra lived a few blocks away— and no one would've dreamed they'd still be standing sixty years later.

But here they were. That's where you'd find the homeless, the hookers, tourists who took a wrong turn, Marines from Twentynine Palms waiting for the last evening ride back to base. All of them looking for a way to get out of the sun.

This was also where Connor Hurst first landed in the low desert, on the bus from Morongo. As he slowed near the driveway where the electric Trailways sign flickered against the cobalt sky, he saw the boy sitting on the low concrete barrier separating the parking lot from the failed business next door.

Interesting. Most Mexicans didn't wear A&F.

Or Connor couldn't remember seeing many who did. But this boy had on a blue shirt that complemented his ropey, smooth brown arms. He was pretending not to notice the slowing Greco & Greco truck, but Connor knew, just knew. He was being checked out.

A boy like this waits for one thing. He slid an arm through his backpack strap, as if he were going to get up and leave.

Connor lowered his window, smiled in the way he'd practiced, which not only created a dimple in his left cheek but also showed off his recently whitened teeth. All this, and at daylight's magic time, too.

"Hey, good lookin,' what you up to?"

Connor knew if you were a poor man looking for another man who was above your station (and it really didn't matter how much above), this kind of cheesy line was acceptable, and this *vato* might not have understood the words anyway.

What was clear was that he understood the intent behind them as he climbed up into the truck cab and sat across from Connor.

He said his name was *George*. Right, George! When you were this hot, it really didn't matter if you lied or what the fuck your name was. He said he came in from Indio, maybe to do some shopping. He lived in a suburb of Indio.

Shopping for what? Indio has suburbs? George was hesitant.

He looked younger, maybe twenty-five, but even that was stretching it. Short but fit, black hair, big dark brown eyes. He was lighter than your average Mex, Connor thought, though dark was never, ever a liability. There was also a scent, earthy, not one he recognized, but quite pleasant. Connor grinned.

"I have to head up to the ridge to check on a property. Come along for the ride?"

George didn't look him in the eye. Instead, he looked down at Connor's thigh, or somewhere in that direction, not as obvious as his crotch, but definitely that general area. He gave a little smile and nodded.

"OK, man," he said.

Connor turned right off Palm Canyon onto Araby, into the hills that led up to Southridge. The more they ascended, the bigger, the better the houses appeared, and the space between them increased. George stretched up to look.

"Who can own this?" Connor thought he asked, but not directed to him. George was thinking out loud; that must be it.

The truck slid over some gravel, raising white dust, marking the end of the public road on a little shortcut Connor knew that took them even higher, through the mountain desert, to nicer houses still.

He told George it was usually the rich old bitch who got the house, the man of the family long dead; all that hard work of making enough cash to buy a place like this killed him off early.

"But they are beautiful *casas*, are they not," George asked. Which he said with such force it wasn't really a question at all; again, it was a state-ment, and an unexpectedly loud one at that.

Connor thought he saw George's upper lip tremble. The temperature rose inside the cab. *Keep your eyes on the road, mister, or you'll never get the prize that's less than half an hour away from you.*

"I'll ask you a second time, there, cowboy: What's your name? Last name too, and don't lie to me."

"George," he said, "Gomes. Gomes with an *s*, not a *z*; we say it softer." Softer.

Gomes. One syllable. He smiled at Connor with his perfectly straight, perfectly white teeth.

Where does a poor Mex like this one get such a perfect mouth, anyway? Connor wondered, turning into the driveway of the house, an approach calculated to impress as much by Connor Hurst as it was by the original 1963 archi-tect. As he slowed on the curve pushing out into an overlook, the Palm Springs lights sparkled below, the lingering glow of the peach sunset fram-ing Mount San Jacinto to the west.

He knew a guy like George Gomes had likely never been to such a layout before, so he'd make it seem like it was something he did every day. Which, in fact, he kind of did, at least in the last year or so.

The house itself floated on walls of glass, stacks of heavy, rosy new tile anchoring the floor here and there, paper-wrapped decks of drywall lean-ing against old walls waiting for an upgrade.

They were inside now, Connor acting like he owned it—he was so fa-miliar with the Greco & Greco projects, he almost did—pushing George mid-spine through the rooms, poking him, heading out to the pool, pull-ing him by the shirt, so fucking hot still, *but there's water in the pool and it's fresh and clean.*

Connor removed his clothes so fast, like he'd rehearsed it, a perfor-mance. A striptease meant to look like it was something else entirely. "Soiled takeoff," he joked, the name of a shitty position he'd once had in a shittier hospital kitchen. That was such a long time ago. Now he was just an everyday working guy needing relief from the tragic desert heat.

He'd had that nice dip in the pool after Sy. Another one couldn't hurt; sometimes even *he* worried about germs on his cock, and he figured the pool chems would kill anything bad. Hell. George Gomes might have is-sues of his own down there: a guy right off the bus!

George stood on the deck, the splash from Connor's dive soaking his white Payless trainers, washing some of the dust off into tiny brown threadlike rivers. He thrust his hands into the front pockets of those amazingly tight jeans, looking around like he was lost.

You're not lost, cowboy, I'm right here. In the pool. Take off your clothes and get in!

George eyeballed the place again as he peeled off his shirt, not quite believing. "Who can have this place?" he asked again.

"Today, dude, you can, dude. Get in *your* pool with me."

Unbelievable, but somehow George had plastered black boxers on under those stretched Wranglers. He sat on the lip of the pool, easing himself into the water with only the slightest ripple.

"George, you can take off the shorts. It's just us."

He ignored this. "I can do this kind of remodel work."

Connor swam over to where George had backed up into one of the pool's corners. "You know, Bob fucking Hope used to live up the street here, right up there."

"Who?"

"Give me your hand."

Connor didn't wait. He slid his hand underwater, a warm knife through soft butter, landing it on George's wrist. Which tensed up right away.

"I want to show you something," Connor said, pulling George with him. They floated like magnets to metal down the side of the pool to an inflow pipe. Hot water pulsed in, though it was hardly needed in the summer.

George giggled as Connor forced his palm against the heated current.

"I think— "

"What?"

"I think you were—"

"Yeah, so?"

"*Sí.*"

Connor moved in closer, pinning George against the scratchy aqua plaster wall. With one hand, he grabbed the deck above for stability. The other went around George's back, pulling him against his chest.

To keep from going under, George had no choice but to put his arms around Connor's neck, their faces an inch or so away from each other. Inevitably, they kissed, George's tongue finding its way deep inside Connor's mouth.

He then disengaged, swimming to the opposite side of the pool, his stroke splashy, juvenile. Connor was right behind him.

Once again Connor's hands were under the water on George, this time on his hips, tugging at his black shorts.

"No."

"Why'd you come up here with me?"

George looked up at the sky, now full of early evening stars. He giggled. "I love this place," he said.

Then he went for it, kissing Connor again, hard on his mouth, his arms tight around the bigger man's neck.

"Yeah, you like it, I really think you do." Connor slid George's shorts off, held them over his head for a second before swinging and hurling them onto the pool deck, hitting the concrete with a nice wet slap, just missing the property line wall.

Then they were out of the pool, hopping over resting tools, paint tubs, two-by-fours, making their way to a room in this empty house where Connor remembered a mattress on the floor.

Which was kind of a lie, as Connor had dragged that mattress up the hill and into this skeleton of a house for those nights when he had no choice but to escape the Grecos or slip toward homicide. Or, a happier outcome, finding a Mexican kid like this one or a Marine with a couple of hours to kill before heading back up to base.

He pushed George down onto the bed and Connor was on top, kissing him, then moving down his chest, brushing each dark nipple with his lips, licking the salty *camino del oro* to his cock, taking it into his mouth.

Gauging George's reaction. His eyes were closed, sometimes half-lidded, out of focus on a point in the ceiling—but he was smiling, like he was having a happy dream.

Enough of that. Over he went, Connor flipping him by the ankles, George's perfect brown ass lit only by the amber light coming in from the outside lights around the pool.

He needed some of that, had to get some of that now. Where's the grease, lotion, some kind of lubrication, and of course, there'd be no fucking condoms between here and Highway 111, he knew that.

But Connor sank his face between George's neck and his shoulder anyway, whispering to the boy, "You want my cock, you want it inside you, don't you?"

He supposed the boy answered, he knew that much English, of course, someone's lying on top of you with a hard-on in your ass crack, and unless you say no it means yes.

■ ■ ■

They lay there wet and naked, staring at the fresh plastered ceiling, though the room was close to pitch-dark now. George moved his head, all that thick black Mexican hair, to rest it on Connor's shoulder, while the not-much-older man tried to remember which renovated place this discarded mattress came from.

"Don't you worry, I'm clean," he said to George, even though he hadn't asked for protection or even seemed aware there might have been an option.

Instead, he nuzzled against Connor and whispered, "I can do this. I can do this kind of work here."

Which surprised Connor, energizing him a little, as he weighed the pros and cons of this new development. "We can always use workers. Sy's always looking for guys," he said.

George kissed him at that little space between earlobe and jawline. "So you will give me a job with your company?"

Connor put his arm around George and pulled him in close. He hadn't planned on this, but it felt right. "We've got an endless list of old folks' houses he wants—and needs—to fix up," he sighed into his ear. "I think you got yourself a job."

3

People always remembered Violet Gamble's high desert house, if not for the exterior stucco cracks (spackled over, the dirty ochre never painted), then for the ample display of heart-stamped breath mints in the emerald glass dish on the small table inside the front door.

The thin, middle-aged redhead's halitosis wasn't helped a lot by the drug use—she couldn't help sampling the product—but here was an effort. She tried to get *everyone* who came through that door to invest in a healthy oral presentation as well.

Perhaps not ever taking responsibility to execute repairs was Vi's method of hiding in plain sight, as she'd never yet been visited by any of Yucca Valley's finest.

It was possible they simply didn't care. Medical marijuana had cut into her business as a small-time seller of weed. Branching out to other, better product would attract the police. Therein lay the problem.

She'd thought Opana would be a natural; it would sell well, she had some connections—older folks, in the main, who wanted to supplement that social security check—and it might pan out. That oxy/Opana retail market, the demand, was already well established in the Morongo Valley. Yet she knew her entry into it would be crushed at once. The trend that so many loyal opiate users would soon graduate to cheaper heroin also made her hesitate.

Vi knew the first rule of drug dealing: If you stand by the window, no buyers come. A breeze whipped up the dust in her yard, rattling the pane. Anaconda Lane was a place folks sought out when they had had enough of being bothered.

My three sons: Which one, if any, will turn out to be useful this time?

Connor, her oldest boy by long-gone Mr. Hurst (who was probably in Texas, but how do you find a man in Texas?), was the dark horse in this race. Down the hill in Palm Springs, *loverboy* pretended to be someone he wasn't, getting close to his bosses in ways she'd rather not dwell on because it made her nervous.

There was the possibility of a windfall there, though it seemed remote, not a sure thing, but better odds than the town casino. Then again, it was potentially a much bigger payday than selling a few ounces of bud would ever be.

Then there was Locker Hurst, the one in the middle, the one who dressed nice to impress people, especially his girls. Head always stuck under the hood of a car, hands flying, fixing whatever needed his touch; somehow the shirt was always clean. Looking so much like his older brother, yet different, smarter, shrewder, showing in that long nose. Vi (she hated that clipped reminder of her white-trash background, her wished-to-be-forgotten Okie heritage) encouraged him to dream big, but bigger for Locker was not much more than a V8.

Right in front of her was the answer. Duane Gamble, her youngest, her dumbest, fair like she was, taking after Mr. Gamble, husband in absentia. Teddy Gamble, likely in Reno (how do you find a man in Reno?), living up to his name, there was little doubt.

"What time those losers tell you they'd get here?" she asked, directed at Duane, who sat at their dining table bagging up product, a table that hadn't seen a proper Sunday dinner in years. No sooner had that thought occurred when she heard a pickup pull up the gravel driveway. *Now, that's how you get something to happen.*

Timbo and Jimbo McLaughlin were twins. She insisted she could tell them apart, but that was a lie, or it was an ability newly acquired every time they met. It was a shame they were crooked, ignorant Marines from the base up the road, but what could you do? Half her customer base was somehow connected to Twentynine Palms, so she needed to shut up and be grateful these two helped out.

Three blond kids around the table: it was like the Cub Scouts all over again, less noise but more danger, working on a misguided Saturday afternoon craft project.

"It's not our fault customers keep deploying out," Timbo said, shrugging his big military shoulders.

Duane caught her eye. This kid always longed for approval. Connor and Locker, her two older boys, had drained her of it and she had no more. "You need to branch out, then," he said.

"Duane's right," Jimbo put in, smiling, showing off his taxpayer-funded straight white teeth. "Keep telling him we got to stop down at the high school, Desert Hot Springs, find that sixteen-year-old poon—"

"Shut it," she said, as a chuckle from behind startled her, making her break the cigarette she'd been waiting to light up.

Locker Hurst leaned against the doorframe, his big bare feet planted on the scratched wooden floor. A peanut butter and jelly sandwich was stuck halfway up his mouth.

"Hey, Locker," said Timbo.

"Hi, Locker," said Jimbo.

"Don't talk with your mouth full," said Vi. "Help your brother."

Timbo counted out the bills for the weed. Duane reached over to grab them, but Jimbo swatted his hand away.

"You don't need my help, do you, Duane?" Locker asked.

Shaking, Vi turned to slap him. She stopped, hearing the faucet creak open outside.

■ ■ ■

His bare back faced her, the faded green waistband of his shorts visible above his jeans.

Connor bent over farther and used the hose to drench his thick black hair. It was hot and windy; she knew the grit from the yard would blow right back in, making this particular procedure necessary again.

Vi lit a fresh cigarette and sat on one of her white plastic patio chairs. "The thing in town?" No reaction, like he didn't even hear her. "That *thing* in town, Connor?" she asked again, louder.

He twisted the spigot and the water slowed to drips. He grabbed a frayed striped towel that hung from a nail on a beam above. "Met a kid. It's all gonna come together, you'll see." He dabbed the perimeter of his face at the hairline. "We're gonna be rich, Sy's gonna put me in his—"

"Bro." Locker slipped out the side door without Vi noticing.

Connor smiled. "Man, I was just coming in to see you."

"Sure."

Connor threw the wet towel at his brother, who caught it with one finger. "I was!"

"Oh, for fuck's sake, Sy did *what*?" Vi rose and flung her cigarette at Connor's feet.

It was like he didn't even hear her, like she wasn't even there.

"Dude, I found the perfect place, old factory shack on 62 out in Joshua Tree," Locker said. "Future home of Locker's Garage."

Vi shook so much she succeeded in twisting the door handle open only on her third try. Car repair, who cares? Back inside, the two Marines and Duane lit up a blunt. Her youngest passed it off to her, and though she might normally decline, as she liked to keep her mind clear—today she inhaled.

Connor had better be right about their plans to share in Greco & Greco's profits. In fact, the more she thought about it, the more perfect answer it needed to be.

■ ■ ■

Jacy Martin was sure there was something not quite right about this old Verna out of Victorville. She was there with her girls, like always, those other bitches from the cold high desert in their wigs and their tracksuits and their training shoes, as if any of them ever ran to anything at all, even to their mailboxes in the senior fucking condo complex.

Montana Grande Casino's background dings and beeps and bells were enough to drown out the cackles and giggles of the hometown crowd—but not when Verna was winning. She won a lot. Verna won more than she should, and he made a mental note to keep an eye on her.

Jacy wore his security hat today, patrolling the family business, he was—like they all did, these Indians who were related and who had to put in hours at the casino. Today he was in that silly purple uniform along with his boy Paco. They walked the aisles and around the perimeters looking for trouble, which was always there if they said it was.

Verna won her jackpot at a quarter-slot bank. Montana Grande Casino in Palm Springs was a beacon to this type of person. Jacy knew that, tried to be grateful of that change in his life that transpired back when he was still in grade school. It was like one day they had nothing but a scratch dirt backyard and the next day they moved into a house where a skinny kid couldn't even count the rooms.

He wanted to be grateful but it usually didn't work. Because they'd see these people, like old Verna and her posse, who got all the money when it should have gone to them.

So he and cousin Paco—a slightly shorter, slightly younger version of himself—stood there while the beautiful Kaya Belardo counted out Benjamins from the old-style cash cart Montana Grande still used.

"What say you and me head up to Vegas tomorrow?" Paco asked, interrupting Jacy's fevered internal resentment tape.

He was breaking one of the most important employee rules. Jacy was not *smiling*. "All the money this place pulls in. Look who gets it."

"That's why we need to go to Nevada, dude; odds are better."

"Fuck Vegas! Andreas should take care of us here."

An older white man, bald but with a bushy gray mustache, turned on the swivel chair at the slot closest to Jacy and Paco. He narrowed his eyes at them, his face sour.

"What you looking at?" Jacy spat.

His beautiful Kaya Belardo must have heard, 'cause she shook her head at him from across that long aisle, where she was still busy handing Verna her payday. For Jacy it was a dreamy slo-mo: the long black hair falling over her eyes, the money sliding between her fingers, the light reflecting off the icy blue glitter she sometimes used on her nails.

But it wasn't a reaction to the white man as much as a nod to him, to remind him that Andreas Alvarado watched and listened to the security monitors—which were everywhere—and from his perch in the executive office, he saw every move, heard every word.

■ ■ ■

Jacy didn't like it much when Andreas Alvarado called him into his office. Which, unfortunately, was too often. The worst part about it was that if Kaya was on shift, like she was right then, she'd be able to see him get screamed at through the soundproof glass.

He hated that! "Question authority" was what the white kids had said back in high school, and he took it to heart. There was no reason fatty Andreas had to be the boss here except for being born into the family he was lucky enough to be born into. Which said nothing about smarts. Nothing about ability. Nothing about how to be decent.

Jacy noticed there was a new picture up on the wall, this one with Andreas shaking hands with the old governor Brown. Right next to that one was the somewhat dusty, somewhat faded photo of a fatter Andreas with Arnold Schwarzenegger. Exactly the same pose, same hands shaking. It must've been a hot day, because in the photo Andreas's shirt was wet around his gut.

Andreas hoped these shots would impress people. Jacy knew he hated politicians of any stripe, but they all had to make nice-nice now that they were in the gambling business.

Goons stood behind him, like guards, which, actually, they were. Not family boys, but men who were tough kids from Indio when they were all teenagers, now with maybe a decade at Calipatria State Prison between them. One black, one Latino; no one could ever accuse this tribe of racist hiring.

Which made Jacy smile, or more accurately, smirk. That would enrage the big man.

"Told you to empty out the pockets, cousin—I don't have all day," Andreas said, closing his metal desk drawer with a loud, screechy slam. Was that supposed to scare him?

"There's nothing in my pockets except for the key to my truck and the key to my place. Nothin' to show *you*."

A subtle nod was all it took for the goons in back to descend on Jacy, who at 146 pounds soaking wet was hardly a match for a little girl like Kaya Belardo, much less these giants.

So he found himself upside down, staring at the stained (but expensive) carpet or Andreas's black slacks, as this was a shakedown of a quite literal variety, the aforementioned keys tumbling out of pocket and under desk; they would need to be retrieved.

As did, of course, the couple of bundles of hundreds and fifties he had in his pockets. How Andreas even knew about these was a mystery, though Jacy suspected—even as the corn bread and the bacon he'd had for breakfast made a serious attempt at also ending up on the floor—that Kaya had sold him out, in some way, perhaps unintentionally.

"Fuckin' put me down!" he screamed, though it came out more as a rasp, inverted as he was.

"Look at that," said Andreas. "Where'd you get this kind of cash, *mijo?*"

■ ■ ■

Jacy wanted to be James Bond, Kaya Belardo thought, or, if not the Englishman in his suit, whatever the Cahuilla equivalent might be. He insisted they meet not at downtown Palm Springs Taco Bell, which would have been convenient and in no way suspicious, but around the big bend in the rocks at the east end of Mesquite. Right inside the res.

The thought of skinny Jacy in a spy-worthy tuxedo made her giggle, which echoed off the walls of the tiny canyon under the sheaf of towering burned brown rocks. She closed her hands over her mouth, the tiny hands that dealt cards and counted cash and even now had the intricate nail painting she'd done on a weekend trip to Oceanside, the thumbnails blue-black, with the rest done up in a wicked leopard print.

She liked being able to do this, to indulge in a beauty treatment, a recent development in her life. Some of the old women on their land shook their heads at the new ventures, at the casinos especially. They were like chattering statues perched around old wood tables, drinking the tea all day long, disapproving of everything, yet stuck in their poverty.

While she waited and laughed and determined the length of time, in weeks, before she'd need that nail touch-up and what kind of outfit would best go with it, back to Oceanside or maybe if it was a good month she'd drive to Newport Beach.

When Kaya was a teenager, those blond beach bitches would give her the evil eye or worse—insist they didn't know how to work with "Indian hair"—but now that they knew she had a casino in the "family," they'd do anything she asked, and, oddly, could do anything with her hair.

That was why money was important, that thing the old women in her family did not understand. Money was the way to get respect. Kaya's female ancestors had to walk these canyons in the blazing heat gathering up mesquite seedpods for that awful Indian cake.

She shuddered at the thought. Her life had been a lucky roll of the dice.

The same ancestors watched over her now, their spirits filling this sacred canyon, which butted up to the baby boomers' trailer park. The tribe had recently installed security cameras at the entrance to the trail. Kaya knew alternative routes; she was able to circle around through the bush, undetected and unseen, to where she could wait for Jacy—literally behind a rock.

Sometimes, like today, it helps to be a shorty, she thought. Of course, it was pushing 115 degrees here (though she was in the shade of that rock), and no one else from the tribe was fool enough to hike out this way past

May. That's why they could meet here; no danger of being spotted somewhere other than the casino.

Meeting anywhere else meant Andreas Alvarado would find out. Kaya Belardo had lived with him now for almost five years. Old enough to be her father, he had money, and that meant respect. He had a college degree, the only man from the res who had one, and now he was the general manager of the casino, its highest paid employee.

So she'd stay with him. Then she started working with Jacy, so close every day. Even though they were distantly related and came up together in the same schools both on the res and then in Palm Springs, she saw something new.

Jacy was sexy in that way Andreas didn't have a clue how to be. The way he looked at her, the way he sometimes moved his hips in the suggestive way, made her get warm, her face even redder than normal. He was poor but he gave her things, and she didn't ask where he got the money at first because she knew it called on hard times to get these things. She wanted to think he was striving for her, and if she couldn't marry him it was worth it for the fun they were having.

She heard a rustle and a cough. You could tell him all you wanted about how to be quiet and discreet, and it—it was like those stereotypes the white folks had about them, like they were good at tracking and sneaking up on shit, and Jacy was about as far from that as anyone she could ever imagine, red man or not.

"There you are," he said, the stupid smile on his face, the bandana he wore for sweat pulled down unexpectedly over his right eye. Gangbanger or dumb Indian, she couldn't decide. Not likely to survive in any case.

"Finally! Goddamn it, Jacy Martin, it's freakin' hot. Why can't you ever be on time?"

He held her, pressing their bodies together, her back scraping on the rock behind her.

Excuses tumbled out: last-minute orders from Andreas, then no gas, broken stoplight, how funny in a dump of a small town like Palm Springs—at least the parts not owned by the family.

"Did you bring me the money?" he asked her, breathless, still holding her close, not letting her go like Andreas would.

Her heart sank like the rocks they used to pitch from the top of the nearby falls into the mountain pool below. Straight to the bottom, floating to an unheard thud.

"You just gave me that Greco check yesterday," she said, measured, slow, a whisper; it might have even been a breeze, if this overheated canyon ever had anything of the sort.

A meaningless gesture on her part, as nothing would stop Jacy in his single-minded determination to find and get money.

"It's for us, baby. It's for our home, for our little spot, that nest," he said, shifting what little weight he had from one foot to the other. Like he had somewhere to get to, like he had to go behind a rock and pee.

"You know what he'd do to me if I got caught?"

He kissed her forehead, each eye in turn. "You won't, Kaya, 'cause you're too good, you're too smart; you and me together, we're so much smarter than Andreas."

He patted the leather bag, her casual purse slung over one shoulder. "It's in here, right? Let's go pay the landlady and spend the rest of the afternoon in *our* condo."

Actually that did seem like a good idea. The other alternative was to go home and wait for Andreas, which she dreaded. Against her better judgment, and almost like watching a movie of herself from a camera placed somewhere on the rocks above, she slid her hand into the purse and felt the neatly folded wad of cash she'd just stolen from the family business. Then again, it wasn't *from* the family business; it was only laundered there.

Maybe that made it all slightly less dishonest.

Jacy finally let her go and rushed off ahead, stashing the bills in his front jeans pocket. Out of the corner of her eye, Kaya detected a flicker. A gray shrike had landed on the pole that supported the camera the tribe hoped would catch illegal hunting or, at the very least, white teenage partiers.

4

Connor Hurst had many secrets. One, which likely nobody—not his women, not his men or even his fucked-up family—would've guessed in their wildest dreams, was that he liked to wear shoes with a heel.

Specifically, nice ladies' shoes with an elevated heel. He owned two pairs. The first was a shiny pair of red platform patent leather pumps with a four-inch heel. These were the shoes he liked to wear around the pool, while also wearing his Speedo. When alone, of course. He'd apply the right amount of coconut oil and rub it on his quads, hamstrings, calves. He loved the definition, the relief of the muscle with the shine of his tan and his dark leg hair. The angle accentuated his calves: A stud in high heels was ten times a stud.

He had to keep these things to himself. Some people—those two Marines, or Sy and Pilar, for instance—would just not understand.

■ ■ ■

Carole Blair Rosen had been a TV star in the '60s, when she was simply Carole Blair. Though eighty-one, she still had one of those faces people thought they knew, even with that small amount of plastic surgery. She always had a glow, too, a tan, but it wasn't too dark; she didn't have that leathery or saggy skin. So she knew some secrets. Like many of the actresses from her era, she still wore her blond hair in the style that made her famous—in this case, a short bob.

Connor tried to recall the name of the series that defined her. She'd told him before but he always forgot. It was so obscure clips hadn't even made it to YouTube. Something about a teacher at an inner-city school—though Carole didn't play the teacher; she played the teacher's odd hippie neighbor.

Which was sort of the inspiration for the other pair of heels he liked—cork wedges, a nice couple of open-toed slingbacks he sometimes wore around the house after a shower, often with a plush terry robe. Carole had planted that seed, showing him a photo of her beaded, counterculture character wearing something similar. The wedges continued as her footwear of choice. He knew she'd be wearing them today.

He smiled at these private thoughts, grateful they were indeed private since he was with the crew—George, with Jimbo and Timbo McLaughlin—as they pulled into the Rosens' drive at their small but classic mid-century home near Ruth Hardy Park.

Carole stood in the doorway. She had waited and watched for them through the big picture window in the living room. Connor knew having young men in her home was the highlight of her week.

Perhaps the short-sleeve Greco shirts reminded her of the Hollywood crews she'd work around at the studio back in the day. Perhaps it was that after fifty-plus years with Harry Rosen, something that didn't fall into the humdrum pattern of ticking off the endless days in the silent desert was simply exhilarating.

"Harry, the boys are here," she yelled back into the house, turning her head. Connor noticed she leaned on a cane today. "I've been waiting for you all morning." She looked him in the eye, which always unnerved him.

"We're running a little late," he said. She turned and swept into the house, pushing the door open wide, her printed mint robe billowing, her wedges making the tiniest squeak. Connor whispered to George, "Newbie, watch what we say and do, OK?"

Carole waited for them to file in, first Connor with George on his heels, the two Marines bringing up the rear. She was the only person he'd ever seen who actually used a cigarette holder—she held it now, though it wasn't lit; Carole told him the doctor insisted she give it up, give quitting one more try.

Her husband, Harry Rosen, was plastered to the plaid recliner in the living room. Connor couldn't remember if he'd ever seen Harry anywhere else, so much so he seemed to be part of the chair itself. He was a few years older than Carole, or at least he looked it. The bald man wore his usual uniform: short-sleeve Hawaiian shirt, black slacks, running shoes. Also per usual, the half-smoked cigar butt in the ashtray on the side table, the stack of *New York Times* at his feet.

"Now, we've had a few problems with contractors in the past, isn't that right, Harry?" she said as she walked by him without stopping.

"That's right," he answered, the entourage walking through a hallway toward the kitchen, their backyard pool sparkling though a window ahead of them.

"I do hope Greco & Greco is an honest company." Carole stopped abruptly at the wall outside the powder room, their destination. "See the bowing, the little bulge here? All that rain last winter, I thought we were going to float away!"

Connor nudged George, who held a clipboard and a pen. "Make sure you get this all down," he said, knowing full well that George wouldn't understand everything—or anything—from Carole or Harry. Timbo snickered.

"New drywall, I think," Carole said, George furiously scribbling, getting with the program, just as Connor hoped he would.

He knew this house would go for a fortune. Sy would be pleased. Once the Rosens found out they could never catch up on the inflated payments they'd signed on to, they'd be dying to sell to the Grecos.

They could move to senior living down valley or find a trailer somewhere; they'd be fine. They'd be just fine.

Carole entered the powder room, a seventies artifact overpowered with rose flocked wallpaper, an avocado toilet and sink.

"There's cracked tile in here, and we need to get rid of those awful colors, please."

Connor nodded and smiled. "I've got some fresh desert olive shades we can show you—"

"And it's so dark. What would you think of a skylight?" Connor, George, Timbo, and Jimbo all looked up at the ceiling, a sad expanse with a single globe light illuminating water stains.

"Sweet," Timbo said.

"Yes—all these things will be taken care of, and I'll personally make sure this job is professional and on time, on budget—"

"We stand behind everything we do," Jimbo added, forcing a smile, not to be upstaged by his nastier twin.

Connor grabbed Jimbo's forearm and squeezed. "Like Jim here says, we stand behind the Greco guarantee."

Carole Blair Rosen was not unintelligent; she caught the tension, then decided to draw it out by lighting up her cigarette from matches stacked in a dish on the toilet cover. She blew the smoke at Connor.

Four men and an old lady in a small powder room and no one talked. George coughed. "*Señora*, door here is crooked," he whispered, running his hand along the edge of the wood.

Connor raised his eyebrows and grinned at his protégé. Carole took another drag on her cigarette. "Young man, I think you're right."

"I'll add that door to our list," Connor said, taking the clipboard from George. "Anything else you find, give us a call—"

But Carole had already left and was floating toward her husband in the living room. "It's going to be so nice, all new for us, Harry!"

Jimbo's big hands landed on George's shoulders, squeezing, shaking. "You're catching on, Georgie," he said.

"He sure is." Connor handed the clipboard back to George, who was being led out of the powder room by Jimbo. "He's one of us now."

Connor nodded to Timbo. "Let's go. By the way, be careful with my bro Duane up at the house—watch him when he counts out for you. He thinks you and Jimbo are slow."

■ ■ ■

Pilar Greco's folks never trusted Sy.

Parents sometimes came in dreams like messengers, gods of the old world, those Aztec gods—warriors, yes, but also the odd cannibal and baby killer. Which made her shudder.

Pilar Greco's father could get away with wearing that kind of Mexican native monumental headdress—he had the features for it, even if he wasn't wearing anything other than a simple sensible suburban shirt and shorts in her dream. She, in turn, took after her mother—small, finely featured, but with the very same jet-black hair, now accentuated a tiny bit with each salon visit.

In her dream, they sat around the pool in the backyard of their Scottsdale home. Mr. Galindez never understood why his Pilar had married an Italian, a Jew Italian, but that was the least of his worries. He was wary of Sy Greco even as he appreciated his better qualities. It was in the eyes; it was always in the eyes.

"You just have to look, look hard, *mija. In the eyes.*"

Such was the memory that surfaced when the nosy *Desert Sun* reporter Nancy Argento called the office. Pilar didn't usually answer the phone; she was distracted after nibbling on a Godiva someone left at reception. Worrying it might discolor her teeth, and what could be more disgusting than little brown bits stuck in dental work?

She was distracted, so she answered the call, and it was this Nancy. Told an impossible tale of deceit by a crazy old bag woman; she must be a stupid writer to believe such a thing. From someone who lived under a bridge!

This reporter Nancy wanted to talk to Sy; he was even there, present in the office. But Pilar was the one who did the talking for them. Sy didn't know when to shut up; he always gave out just a shred more information than he had to. Information that could and would come back and bite them both in the ass.

Pilar knew this Nancy was fishing, but there wasn't going to be anything ever caught on that line. Greco & Greco invested in classic mid-century homes; what was strange about that? Everyone with a little bit of cash was doing the same thing—the new century's version of a baby boomer gold mine.

So there was no excuse when she got a little flustered, and who could blame her, anyway? There seemed to be a conflict of interest, Nancy Argento said. What was a realty company doing in the home-remodeling business, anyway?

Whenever Pilar took a difficult call like this she focused on the photo framed on her desk, the one of her and Sy with their son, Angel Greco, sitting down in front, taken just a few weeks before he died. If she'd just held on to him like in the photo, her hand on his shoulder, squeezing his bony twelve-year-old flesh. His hair had been as dark as hers, but it had a little curl in it, courtesy of his dad's DNA.

Don't ever let go; don't ever let that beautiful boy leave you.

Across the office, Sy stared, his mouth open, as if to ask, *Why are you still on this call with this person, this person who wants to destroy us?* She wanted to scream at him, slap him: *She knows, you idiot; she's on to us!*

But instead, she hung up; mid-sentence, she hung up on Nancy Argento, *Desert Sun* reporter. Pilar felt detached from herself as her shaking hand dropped the receiver back into its cradle; it was as if she were watching one of those old-style dramas unfold in slow motion on TV.

Just as quickly her stomach sank to her ankles. Realizing what a stupid mistake that was. How she was not cool, not calm, not collected. So glad her father, Mr. Galindez, was not there to see her being the bad business-woman, the one whose company would be destroyed because of that lapse in judgment.

She would go to the ladies' room, put herself together and call Nancy back. They were both professionals, after all. They'd come to an understanding.

■ ■ ■

Pilar resisted driving by the Las Palmas intersection where Angel's skate-board had met the Range Rover. Sometimes she'd park there on her way home from Greco & Greco, if she had something to think about or if she was merely avoiding Sy. Despite the violence of what had happened, it was a quiet residential street. Maybe the boy's essence still hovered there, his spirit. He might give her comfort, might give her an answer, even.

To pressing questions.

Like, for instance, if she should divorce Angel's father. It was true: He preferred Connor Hurst to her, but the other truth was that she, in her own way, preferred Connor to Sy. So there they were.

She smiled, a rarity these days. She watched herself through the rear view, as much to look out for other neighborhood kids being reckless—she would scare them with the tale of the death meted out here—as to check makeup. Lipstick needed a slight touch-up. The formulas still weren't re-sistant to this Palm Springs brand of insane and constant inferno.

Pilar knew her feelings were all wounded pride, and misplaced pride at that. They had a good thing going, she and Sy Greco, so intertwined at this point that even the mere thought of dividing it all up exhausted her.

No, really, the alternative she and Connor had planned for him was vastly superior to any boring no-fault California divorce.

She should get home, check on the orchids. It was their day to be tended to. She glanced at the dashboard: 114 degrees! She'd brought every pot of them inside at this time of year, but supposed one or two were for-gotten in that spot in back of the pool.

The front door was open. Pilar hated it when Marina left it this way, espe-cially when it was so hot. She'd never be far, and always intending to close it after doing whatever it was she was doing—but it was this short delay that made Pilar Greco think the Ukrainian woman was more than a tiny bit passive-aggressive.

She wouldn't give her maid satisfaction by appearing to notice. Not today. The red floor tiles were shining; she'd give her that. Somebody was in the pool—the little slaps of water against concrete echoed all the way into the foyer.

"Sy?" she called out, though if he were in the pool he couldn't hear. Frolic time with Connor had probably happened earlier; she'd give Sy that, he was considerate enough not to throw their affair in her face.

No answer. Pilar went to the bar, where she knew there was still a glass of that Montevina pinot they'd opened the day before. Something nice and cool and medicated for a hot afternoon.

As she took a sip, Marina appeared in the doorway leading to the kitchen. This woman never smiled. Had she ever seen Marina Boyko with anything other than that flat, boring lip line? Not that she could recall. If nothing else, this was predictable, and that had value—a lot of value.

"Mr. Greco outside, ma'am," Marina said, giving an old Bauer turquoise vase on the side table a little quarter turn.

"I thought that was him in the pool. Is he—"

"He is alone, Ms. Greco. There is no other person out there today."

Everyone knew the elephant in this room was Connor Hurst. Of course she had seen them, and of course she knew: Madame was fucking the young man who lived in the pool house; so was Master.

It had become clear that Marina was not immune to this curious Eastern prejudice against homosexuals. As humorous as this provincial way of thinking might be, it was to Pilar's clear advantage to have the maid on her side.

"I suppose I should check the orchids—I don't think William moved all of them out of that heat," Pilar said.

"He told me he got them all," Marina said, her Slavic nose elevated, the way it always got when she thought a challenge was being leveled. Always keep them guessing; that's what Rodrigo Galindez would say, especially when they're beginning to feel a little too comfortable.

"Of course he *said* that," Pilar answered, not waiting for any further reaction but stepping out of the open sliders onto the patio. Where, as it happened, she saw one of her orchid pots pushed back against the high wall on the far side of the pool.

Her husband was oblivious as she moved around him to retrieve the burned plant. Her intention had been to dump it in the flower bed there.

At the last second, she threw it on the concrete decking in front of her, smashing the pot, scattering the dirt.

This, Sy noticed. He slowed his crawl and grabbed the lip of the pool at the opposite end from where she stood.

"Pilar?"

He sounded alarmed. Good. "These fucking dendrobiums! I told William to take them *all* out of the yard."

"Did you write it down?" he asked, pulling himself part way out of the water. "You know it works better when he has all tasks on a paper he can look at."

She kicked at the dirt with her toe, which only succeeded in spreading it wider over the tiles.

"This is such a mess. *Everything* is such a mess."

Sy laughed, coughing up a tiny bit of the salty pool water he must've swallowed. Laughing at her, at her frustration. She picked up a sharp piece of the broken clay pot, hurling it at him.

It missed its mark by feet, not inches. Which made Sy laugh even more.

Pilar's head was about to explode, the heat and anger a dangerous combination.

"Relax, get your glass—you *did* pour something for yourself, I'm sure," he said.

She'd left the wine inside. Marina had likely removed it, even though she'd know damn well Pilar would finish every last drop. "You're swimming alone," she said, more a question than a statement, another dig.

"Like every damn afternoon of my life," he said. Pilar almost turned to steal a glance at the pool house in the back, where that object of their affection lived, and perhaps was, right this second.

Connor, in the shower, washing any remaining traces of Sy from his body. Connor, taking a late afternoon nap, only vaguely aware his benefactors were arguing outside his door, lying naked, faceup on the pewter-colored duvet she'd bought for that room.

Pilar had a difficult time wrapping her head around the idea that both she and her husband were sleeping with this young man. In particular, she had a hard time with the imagery of body parts and openings and secretions of one sort or the other. Which they now shared. She didn't like to dwell on it.

She'd be angry instead. "Why do you always act like I'm some sort of idiot?"

Sy sat there in the shallow end of the pool, his chest meeting the waterline just below his nipples. Whatever else she could say about him, he looked pretty good, pretty tight for a man who'd turned sixty. He squinted at her, as much an attempt to focus as it was to avoid the sun.

There was disappointment in those eyes, judgment, that feeling she always got, had always gotten, and not so different at all from one she got from the senior Mr. Galindez. *Same old story; it will be better when he's gone.*

"Look at all this," he said, sweeping his hand up out of the water. "You have this great life, Pilar, and you don't even have to be a wife."

It was statements like this that secured her belief, that, indeed, a younger man like Connor was the answer to this kind of total shit. He looked up to her. She liked that; she wanted more of it.

Sy wasn't finished. "Don't be that woman who tosses pebbles. You're that bitch who steals houses from old ladies—remember that."

■ ■ ■

It unnerved Nancy Argento to be sitting at a picnic table under the extended neck of the giant brontosaurus statue at Cabazon.

Stress factors: unrelenting freeway traffic; the wind, hot today, which also never let up; the constant possibility of an earthquake along the San Andreas Fault nearby, which would send the steel-and-concrete dinosaur crashing down upon her.

Plus, there was Ernst, her sometimes boyfriend, depending on whether or not the current golf tour wanted to visit a list of courses in Palm Springs. It did, but he didn't want to see her so much, he'd said. He needed his Euro-space. Besides, it was July, and he couldn't take the temperature. That, and she'd had that reading at Blue Collie bookstore in Phoenix; only about fifteen people showed. Only one person bought a copy of *A Death at Smoketree.*

Fine. What did she need that kind of aggravation for, anyway? For a second she thought she might miss those midwestern guys with their football jerseys and their sincerity after all. Maybe she'd move back to Ohio.

And maybe not. Stories like the one unfolding—with the Grecos screwing over nice old retired ladies—were hard to come by in the rusty, depopulated neighborhoods of Cleveland, where people like this had long been fucked and forgotten.

Yet there was urgency to this story. She'd always been good with intuition, and that extra sense screamed at Nancy, telling her that editor Hart was not happy. That the Third Coast promise of an edge she'd brought so well initially was faltering; that it was in fact empty.

She hoped her hunch was right this time, or she'd be back in Ohio before the snow fell. She'd met with Ginny McFadden twice more, each time with a new and more expensive bottle of whiskey to help things along. The old lady didn't disappoint: she knew of others in the same situation—homeless women who couldn't pay Greco & Greco bills—whom she'd met at the daily senior lunch she took at the Mizell Center in Sunrise Park. A pattern was developing.

The chattering of a newly arrived little family at the picnic table next to her disrupted her thoughts. They were textbook WASP, striking because one didn't see that kind of thing that much anymore, especially not here in Southern California. Dad, mom, a boy and a girl. Surely, there was a golden retriever at home, a Buddy or a Jake or a Sparky. The little blond girl tossed French fries for desert birds gathering for their own free lunch. Nancy was about to complain about this when behind the child a black Greco & Greco SUV pulled in to park.

It had to be Pilar Greco in the passenger seat, same long black hair as in the website photo. She stared straight ahead, as if looking right through Nancy. Her lips moved. The driver was a short but nice-looking Latino kid. He left the vehicle running as they finished whatever conversation they were having.

■ ■ ■

Nancy felt relieved she wasn't the only woman who wore heels out in the desert in the middle of July.

Pilar Greco joined her under the dinosaur. Wearing oversized sunglasses, she nodded toward the SUV, which still hummed; the driver had to keep the air-conditioning running.

"That's George, a kid new to us. Seems like a nice boy, hoping I can trust him. I left our bank deposit in an envelope on the car seat," she said.

Interesting. *Entering overshare territory.* "Do you think that's wise?"

"My intuition on these types of things is usually right on." She turned to smile at Nancy, opening her clutch purse and pulling out cigarettes.

"You're not going to smoke at me, are you?"

One thing Nancy had to admit about Pilar Greco—the woman had a statue-like poker face, here enhanced by the opaque sunglasses, which were becoming more disconcerting by the minute. She pulled out a cigarette and lit it. Inhaling death.

"What's the problem? We're here in the wide-open desert, fresh air for your nice little lungs all around. I lead a stressful life. You'd smoke too; *you would.*"

Shut up, you entitled cunt. The words tumbled over and over in Nancy's head, behind what she hoped was that pleasant, professional smile. Time was when she'd articulate such a thing without a blink, hence her history of job-hopping. With luck, she'd get to stay at the *Desert Sun*, if she could let it lie when she needed to.

"It may seem OK now, but bad habits catch up with people. Ask my father. Also, that kid's real name is *George*? I'm calling bullshit."

Pilar turned her head away to exhale. "That's what he told us his name was," she said. "He has an ID— Look, I'm a considerate person. Not as bad as you seem to think. Again—I want to apologize for hanging up on you. It was one of those awful days; we all have them at work. Don't you, Ms. Argento?"

"Nancy. Call me Nancy." It was at least pleasant to talk to someone who appeared to be a successful businesswoman, even if she did turn out to be a criminal. Someone who did not insist on shot after shot of booze to simply talk.

George in the SUV opened the door and stood out in the sun, stretching his arms over his head, yawning. He leaned against the vehicle's black finish, which didn't seem to burn him. There was something a little off about him, compared to the usual Mexican day workers Nancy saw all the time in this desert. Something more studied, intentional, deliberate.

"Why did you have me come all the way out here? I'm glad we could meet in person, but Cabazon?"

Pilar took another long drag off the cigarette, again making a show of blowing it away from the table. "You said it couldn't wait, and we're repping some property out here, so there wasn't much choice if you wanted to meet today."

The WASP family, done with their burgers and sodas, rose to leave. They did not take their garbage with them. They left the tubs and papers and cups sitting there and disappeared into the back parking lot, behind the adjacent and giant Tyrannosaurus rex.

"Look at that. I don't know what's wrong with people these days," Pilar said, staring up at the underside of the beast shading them. "I figured everybody likes dinosaurs."

Nancy smiled. "Repping property out here? It's a whole lot of desert. What is this, reservation land?" There was that inscrutable smile again. Nancy pulled an envelope out of her bag and placed it between them on the concrete table. She thought she caught the tiniest quiver at the furthest edge of Pilar's mouth.

"Home remodel contracts. Copy of a tape—a little conversation I had with Ginny McCadden. I thought you'd be interested. Go ahead."

Pilar undid the little clasp and glanced inside, then put the envelope back on the table.

"Old ladies in Palm Springs like to tell stories. Our *lawyer* would say she's got dementia. Which she does—if you met her, you know."

Nancy's hand was still inside her bag, where her fingers petted the weird orange hair of that troll doll charm she'd lashed to the camera strap. She might tremble if they were on the table. She didn't want Mrs. Greco to see that.

"There are more ladies, more stories," Nancy said.

Pilar nodded, then surprised Nancy by removing the big sunglasses. She had stunning brown eyes—*if I had those I'd never cover them up.*

"Look . . . Nancy," she began. "I'd want to know exactly what it is Sy is being accused of by these women, because that's the last thing we'd ever want." She actually smiled. "I'm going to help you."

"Good, because I've made some calls up to Sacramento, real estate regulation, those people. At minimum it's a serious ethics violation; at its worst it's fraud—"

Pilar's cell phone rang, the ringtone the obnoxious twang of a pop song passed off as a bona fide country hit. She stood and walked down dinosaur toward the animal's crotch, where its genitalia would be if there were such things.

George stood against the SUV. He'd put on a wide-brimmed gardener's hat, pulling it down to shade his eyes. He was watching her and tipped it when Nancy looked over at him.

Whatever call this was, Pilar was engrossed. Stalling, Nancy thought. It's that simple: *Get off the damn phone.* She wasn't going to sit there and wait; perhaps the kid knew something. Nancy walked over to him. He crossed his arms but otherwise didn't move.

"*Hola,*" she said, trying out her pathetic but serviceable Spanish. George nodded.

"I speak English, OK?"

Not what was expected. So: "The people who own these dinosaurs here are Christian fundamentalists who believe humans lived alongside these things just a few thousand years ago," she said. "Crazy, eh?"

He didn't react, and she wasn't sure he understood her. Pilar by now had raised her voice. "They're not too keen on illegals, Mexicans, gays. Especially illegal gay Mexicans."

He nodded. She thought there might have been a quick flash of anger, but it dissipated almost as soon as it came. He was good, very good.

"That was a joke, by the way. *Usted no sabe lo que estoy hablando, ¿verdad? ¿De dónde?*"

The boy frowned and looked away. His eyes followed Pilar, and Nancy knew he hoped she'd return right this second, before she could ask any more questions.

■ ■ ■

"Don't worry about her," Connor said.

George stood at the side of the pool at the empty house in Southridge. He and Connor had agreed swimsuits of any kind were unnecessary, even inconvenient. Inevitably, when they got together they'd soon find themselves naked.

A goal was to fuck in every room of the house. He'd never even dreamed of being in a mansion like this, much less living in one. That's right, Alma Gomez, Chuy and Jesse, a place where a Gomez or a Gomes didn't have to bend over to look at himself in the crooked mirror between his brothers' bunk beds, a place where a rasping air conditioner didn't drip on his pillow while he tried to get some rest.

Connor worked it out so George could watch over the place during renovations. There wasn't much there other than a mattress and an old patio table and some plastic chairs, but what did a person need anyway, when you had a man like Connor around and a swimming pool with a view such as this?

"Don't worry about Mrs. Greco, either," Connor said, from his usual spot in the corner of the pool where he could rest his arms over the lip of the deck. "You do a good job for her. You *always* do a good job."

George didn't jump into the pool. He wondered where he would go when this was finished. After a taste of this, he couldn't go back to Mecca, no matter how much his mother complained or his brothers cried. George missed his family too, but it was for the best; this would help them out. It would just take some time.

"*Gracias,*" he said, almost a whisper. He'd tried to leave the family before, though he hadn't mentioned it to Connor. Almost a year earlier, a stupid job washing old *maricones'* heads before their haircuts at a salon off Palm Canyon. The owner let him sleep in a storeroom in back. It ended when George stopped having sex with the boss.

"You sound like you don't believe me, George," Connor said. "A guy like you can make some money here. You know how many rich people are out in this desert?"

George shrugged and looked away, toward looming Jacinto, where the nearly full moon appeared to be resting on the summit. "You tell me— lots, you say lots."

"Let me explain for you *again* how it works. We collect the money from the old folks and it goes to the Indian guys. They keep some for themselves and then send Sy Greco the rest. It's like *free money*, since you're not officially doing the work and you don't really exist—"

"But I *am* here. Right here, man! If I don't 'exist,' like you say, how do I become American?"

Connor swam over to where George stood and grabbed his ankle, but George wouldn't have it. He kicked his hand away, backing up.

"Look around you," Connor said. "Look at this place."

"Is not enough."

"You want to cut some fat fuck's grass for the rest of your life?"

"No, of course—"

"Then take it. Or you can always go back to Mexico."

"I do the work, *honest*, I get paid, *honest*."

Connor floated on his back away from the edge of the pool, away from George.

"You can always go back to Jalisco," Connor said. "You know, that's a great idea—I'll take you back to that dirty bus. Where I found your dumb ass."

"I'll stay till I find other job, OK?"

Connor didn't say anything further, but swam back to the other side of the pool, as far away from George as he could get. It would be so easy to slip into the water and go to him, get all wrapped up in those big arms and start the sex for all night—like they usually did.

Instead, George tied a thick blue towel around his hips and turned away. Walking back into the house, he heard a slap and figured it was Connor punching the surface of the water. *Bueno*. Let him wait.

He entered the special bathroom just inside the door, which was for the pool area only, for the guests of the master when they visited and had to pee. He took a cigarette from a pack that was on the marble counter and lit it, staring at himself in the mirror, fixing his thick hair with his fingers.

Connor's watch was lying there. He picked it up and watched the second hand moving around the dial, *tick-tick-tick*. He didn't want to go back outside too soon.

5

Of course they spent the night together anyway. George thought Connor probably did love him; he certainly liked having the sex. When they kissed they didn't argue. George craved being held in those big strong arms every night and also figured it was part of the bargain allowing him to sleep in this empty mansion. Then there would always come the minute, anyway, every night, when exhaustion set in and no more English could be understood.

Connor was asleep. His chest rose and fell against George's back. Things were going so well now. He'd even completed the task Pilar Greco had asked of him, her test, to see if he was a thief.

George had brought the cash bag into the office after the Cabazon visit. Daniel Pearson, the company administrative assistant, sat at a desk in front of this atrium desert flora exhibit, which had one plant that wasn't a plant at all.

Daniel was one of the few people George had seen in Palm Springs who bothered to dress up for work, even when it was summer and every day turned out to be 115 degrees by the afternoon. Today he wore a blue bow tie and a white shirt. Tall and skinny and blond, he looked like an overgrown Catholic schoolboy.

He took a key and opened the center desk drawer, removing a slip of paper. He grabbed the cash bag, turned on his chair, and rolled it over to the cactus array. At the fake green saguaro, he pulled open a trap door— which George hadn't realized was there.

He stopped. "Don't watch me. What's wrong with you?" Daniel asked, narrowing his eyes at George, who stood there, pretending to mind his own business. "Turn around."

George laughed. "Don't be crazy, man. I'm not watching you."

With his flat, blank expression, Daniel stared at George, looked him up and down, then blinked a couple of times and let out a loud sigh. He turned back to his cactus task. *This man, he's so dramatic,* George thought.

But his nice shirt and bow tie couldn't hide everything George could see. The paper held the lock codes; that was certain. There was a lot of green in that safe that wasn't part of the fake cactus at all.

Daniel's desk phone rang.

His hands shook as he transferred the bundles of bills from one cash bag to another.

Then, while the phone still rang, getting louder with every ring, Sy's voice boomed over the intercom: "Danny, can you come in here for a second?"

"Oh, crap!" he shouted, knocking the safe door closed with one hand while tossing the now-empty cash bag back to George. Daniel rolled his chair back up to the desk, finally answering the phone: "Greco & Greco, how may I direct your call?"

Sy was on the intercom again. "Danny! Where the fuck are you?"

Daniel knocked over the pencil holder in his hurry to grab a pen. "Right, OK, let me connect you," he said into the phone. He pushed a button and hung up, grabbed a notebook and rushed past George to Sy's office.

George smiled when he looked down and realized Daniel had left the key in the desk drawer's lock, its metal chain lightly scraping the edge.

■ ■ ■

George's thoughts raced, new possibilities of money coming his way, bouncing off the walls and ceiling of the giant Ralph's grocery, exceeded in pace only by Jacy Martin's constant babble.

Sy had sent the two of them to pick up water and snacks for the various Greco & Greco project work crews.

At night in the summer, Ralph's wasn't too crowded, the usual stray tourists and senior citizens, two of whom George recognized as that glamorous Carole Blair and her older man, Harry Rosen.

Harry pushed the grocery cart; Carole hooked her pinky finger, topped with a glittery ring, around the wire frame at the front of the basket, not so much pulling as acting as a show-off rudder. She wore another one of those long loose dresses sold by the road in Jalisco, but that no one down there would ever put on. This one was orange.

"Let's find those canned tomatoes, Harry," she said. George could hear her from the opposite end of the enormous aisle. "They got that lyco crap, you know, we need it for your prostate, honey."

Jacy didn't appear to recognize the Rosens. If he did, he didn't say anything. They were on a collision course and would meet head-on unless someone turned around. George hoped this was one of those times when all Mexicans looked alike to white people. It didn't help that he and Jacy still wore their company T-shirts.

Carole pulled red cans from the shelf. She put one in the cart, handed the other to Mr. Rosen.

"Lyco*pene*. But I like the ones from Whole Foods better," Harry said.

We could turn this cart around—now—but the noise would draw attention.

"You're too lazy-ass, George, come on," Jacy said. The bulk water bottles they needed were stacked at the end of this aisle. Jacy homed in on them, his skinny shoulders hunched over the cart, his eyes focused on the goal, a loco animal eyeing its prey. It was inevitable they would pass the Rosens, if not hit them.

"Tomatoes, sha-ma-toes! We can't afford to go there with all the remodeling we're doing; you know that, Harry," she said.

Jacy raced his cart right past the Rosens. George followed as quickly as he could, but it wasn't fast enough.

Carole scrunched up her nose when she saw him, like she needed a detail to focus on. "Speak of the devil," she muttered. He heard her and he understood.

Now the Rosens were following *them*.

Jacy still hadn't said anything; maybe he truly didn't know who they were. George could hear every word.

"What do I know of such things?" she asked. "I suppose the Greco & Greco bills are fair."

Harry Rosen coughed. "Bullshit! They think we're stupid because we're old."

George hung back while Jacy charged ahead with the now full cart, a direct line to the cashier and beyond to the dark parking lot. The Rosens had stopped. Carol tossed two more tomato cans into their cart. George stood inside the adjacent aisle, listening.

"Now, Harry—let me say something. The work's almost done; we got that nice loan from Mr. Greco—it's all going to look so modern!"

Before George could move out of the way, the Rosen cart lurched around the corner. He and Harry made unavoidable eye contact. "I don't like being taken advantage of!" Harry said, his eyes bulging at George.

"*Perdón*, please," George whispered, turning as fast as he could to follow Jacy out of the store.

At the Greco truck, George grabbed one end of the shrink-wrapped water-bottle case Jacy was trying to heave into the back. "I thought you got lost," Jacy said, wiping his nose on his shirtsleeve.

It was one of those nights when the winds from out of the Gorgonio Pass made a southerly detour into Palm Springs proper, sending dried palm fronds flying from their high anchor to unsuspecting targets below. Paranoid that he was, Jacy had parked in the alley beside Ralph's, where the only vehicle was theirs, an obvious target for these fronds—which no one could see coming anyway, since it was pitch black now.

None of them hit the truck. Instead, imminent danger came in the form of old Harry Rosen.

Who appeared in front of them, standing with his spindly arms locked to his sides. The glamorous Carole Blair was nowhere to be found.

"Boys, I want to talk to you," he said.

Finally, Jacy recognized him. Somewhere in his thick head a light switched on.

"Can't you see we're in a hurry? And this wind, it sucks, man."

But Harry stood there, his balled-up fists resting on his hips, standing as tall as he could. George could smell the trace of a cigar from the man's ridiculous floral print shirt.

"I got another bill yesterday from that Mr. Sy Greco," he said. "Something we already paid. I think your boss likes to steal from retired people!"

He was loud. In fact, his voice could be heard even over the wind. Where was his wife? Had he left poor Carole in the store?

George scanned the area to see, but they were alone—though at any moment a car or somebody with a grocery cart might roll around the corner.

He laid a light hand on Harry's rounded shoulder. "Mr. Rosen, *please*, not so angry, OK?"

The old man pushed him off. "I will not be quiet, you little brown *feygele*!"

George backed off, confused; he pulled himself up into the back of the truck to stack their purchases.

"Fucking get lost," Jacy said.

Harry pressed to within an inch of Jacy's face. "We'll see who gets lost!"

A spark shot up George's spine, because he knew you didn't do this kind of thing to the Indian. You never knew quite where you stood, or what would happen.

And what happened was that Jacy, in one quick microsecond, pushed Harry. Pushed him back with the full fury of both hands slapped against his bony octogenarian chest. Harry reeled backward, lost his balance and fell.

Onto a concrete parking curb, headfirst. A dark halo of blood radiated from his face. His eyes were open. He didn't move.

George dropped the last case of water bottles onto the truck bed (where they landed with a thud) and jumped down onto the asphalt. Jacy stood there, frozen. George bent to get a good look at Harry.

"Oh my God, Jacy. We get him to the hospital!"

"Shut up and help me," Jacy said. He tried to lift Harry by his shoulders, but the old man was too heavy. "Help me!"

George thought Harry was probably dead, but how could he know for sure? They managed to get him into the back of the pickup. Blood was everywhere, on their hands, on their pants. Jacy threw a rain tarp over Harry.

"We take him to the hospital," George repeated.

Jacy leaned against the tailgate, catching his breath. He wiped a smear of blood onto the back of his jeans. "Dumbass. It's too late for that."

■ ■ ■

Jacy said they'd both be thrown away in jail forever if they called *anyone*—hospital, police, tribal council—anyone. Even though it was an accident. They had to get rid of Harry; they had to make him "disappear."

So they picked up shovels at the supply shed in back of Greco & Greco, dropping off the water and other supplies in the process. The Palm Springs light-pollution ordinance was their friend, the expected inky dark helping them disguise the cargo now driven out into the desert.

Jacy stopped far enough away, though the lights of the desert cities were still visible as a thin white line on the horizon. It seemed to George that he and Jacy dug for hours, until the black sky began to turn gray, when they finished covering Harry Rosen with sand.

On a short rise near the truck a lone coyote stopped to watch, then trotted off. George leaned against the smooth wood of the shovel handle. Had they buried Harry deep enough? He watched as Jacy jumped up and down, doing a little dance on the fresh grave to pack the earth. Then he giggled.

"What?" Jacy asked.

"That's funniest thing I've seen all day," George said, laughing out loud.

Jacy stomped over to the truck and tossed his shovel in the back. "Shut up, George. You must have a real sweet thing going down in Mexico to talk like that. I cannot believe what a fuckup you are."

George brushed the wetness from his eyes. "He left Señora Rosen back there, in the parking lot?"

■ ■ ■

One thing Nancy Argento hadn't gotten used to in her short time in California was the odd habit the state's residents had of sitting in their cars. In Ohio, for most of the year, to sit in a car for any length of time required the engine running and the heat *on*.

Then again, she knew that because of this common practice, she wouldn't attract attention if she didn't move till she was absolutely ready. So she sat there, parked at an angle on Arenas Road, parked there in her silver Focus—which at least was new, a great deal from a friend of her boyfriend Ernst's who sold cars out on Perez Road.

Yes, she sat in the car, but with the AC on. *It's the anti-Ohio,* she thought. She'd gotten her triple-shot skinny latte from the Laotian lady (she made a mental note—ask her what her name is; be *friendly*, Nancy; try, try to be part of the town) with the espresso cart, but needed to pick up the dream book from the minimart on Arenas.

The dream book, aka the *New York Times*, was her journalism porn. She turned its pages, committed bylines and beats to memory, fantasized what a day would be like working out of 242 West Forty-First Street in midtown Manhattan. She whispered to herself, "Nancy Argento with the *Times*; I have some questions." Tried that on for size, that seductive opening. Or she'd toss her hair to the side and smile at herself in the rear view, pretending she was on the phone: "Tell him it's Nancy Argento from the *Times!*"

Here on Arenas in the small-town desert, no one would care if they saw this. A woman talking to herself, alone in her car, AC running: People would assume she was on her phone. Or that she had a drug problem. Perhaps both.

Here on Arenas in the tiny gay center of Palm Springs, no one paid much mind to a straight blond girl who was almost thirty. Here she could sip her latte and look at her porn. An added bonus were the giant tamarisk trees, which provided glorious shade.

Truth was, there would be little foot traffic here anyway, on an August day like this where it was already pushing 100 before noon. But the one young man she saw was someone she'd already met.

Dinosaur boy!

What was George Gomes doing walking into Hunter's Bar at this time of day? Being Pilar Greco's flunkie *had* to be a full-time job.

Nancy went in, still channeling what it would be like to be the reporter from the *Times*, even if she had to hesitate before saying, "It's Nancy from the *Desert Sun*."

The empty street belied the activity inside Hunter's. Nancy assumed there had to be a rear parking lot she was unaware of, because the U-shaped bar was just about full.

She checked her mobile once more for the time—it was before noon, 11:24 A.M. to be exact. Yet the room didn't give off that kind of sad desperation alcoholic daytime bars often did. God knows she'd been in a few of them in Cleveland, the stink of spilled whiskey and disinfectant impossible to forget.

Then again, Hunter's was bipolar: it might be toasted tourists, drunk locals and misguided elder queens in the morning, but the place put on the glitter at night as the preferred dance hall for all of young Palm Springs, regardless of orientation. Ted Ligett had taken her there a couple of times on Saturday nights, and she'd had fun.

Nancy glued herself back to the wall in the shadow of a video game machine. She'd brought in her coffee and the paper, pretending to read but actually watching George, who was now behind the bar.

He'd changed into a tight black tank top and was hanging on every word—every word she couldn't make out—of an older, taller black man who sported a Hawaiian shirt and a bushy mustache.

You don't see that every day, she thought. *It's so seventies.*

George was washing, rinsing, stacking glasses and setting up bottles. So—he was working here. Interesting.

One of the reasons Nancy was so curious when she saw him was the news about the missing Harry Rosen. It was Ted's assigned story—but she'd seen the local TV minute, their on-air rivals from down in Palm

Desert, which began with a static shot of the Rosens' house. There was a Greco & Greco truck parked on the street *right there.*

Rosen's hysterical wife didn't know what to think, but it came out that Harry had been diagnosed with Alzheimer's, though quite recently, within the month. He might have simply walked off somewhere and would turn up. The shot ended with a bland look of concern on the face of the six P.M. spray-tanned anchor.

Only problem was, walking off when every summer day featured cloudless weather at 115 degrees could be deadly. She wondered if George Gomes had an opinion, one way or the other.

"Guess it's time to throw this one out," Nancy said, sliding the paper coffee cup across the bar to where George stood.

He looked up at her and blinked. His eyes got wide—with, what was it, panic? Or surprise at a young woman in this late morning mix?

"I can do just so much coffee," she said. "But I always kind of liked that caffeine screwdriver mimosa buzz."

He didn't say anything. For a dim room awash in ever-cooler air-conditioning currents, George had a surprising amount of sweat on his brow.

Finally: "It's my first day," he said.

She was ready to ask about his "remodeling" duties when his boss— Darren, according to the name tag—slid back into view.

"What can I get you, beautiful?" he asked, licking away errant mustache hairs on his upper lip.

He turned with a nod to make the mimosa (on special today!), so she was left with the empty corner of the bar. *Are you actually going to drink this, Nancy, before noon?*

George pretended not to pay attention, consumed as he was with his dishwashing task. He'd pick up a dirty glass from the right side of the sink, plunge it into a vat of soapy water where an automated brush would scrape away the grit, then rinse it off and place it on a towel to his left. Oddly mechanical but sensual.

"So, George, tell me: You know this old guy, this Mr. Rosen, who's missing?"

He didn't stop his washing ritual; if anything, she thought he might have speeded it up.

"Guess he and the wife were having some nice home remodeling done, by none other than your *other* bosses, Sy and Pilar Greco."

She suspected he didn't miss a trick, but even Nancy Argento, cracker-jack reporter, was surprised by how quickly he answered.

"I don't know what you talking about. Guys like me look the same to people like that, right?"

"So you *do* know them—that's what you're telling me?

"I never said." He looked around for Darren, who had left the area, then leaned in to Nancy. "Please, *señorita*. My first day here; they will fire me."

Seconds later—though it seemed endless—the bartender returned with Nancy's drink. George resumed his washing, refusing further eye contact with her.

She took a sip. The champagne in the drink tickled the tip of her nose, sending a calming wave from the top of her head down to her ass. She settled in on the stool, anchoring herself.

She'd have a little fun with George, see how far she'd get. She told him it was common knowledge he was working at the Rosens' the day Harry went missing.

He gripped those cocktail glasses tighter. But he told her no, he didn't know who these people were. Never heard of them. "We work at so many houses," he said. "All of them, every single one, is owned by an old white person." All the *chicos* looked the same to them; after all, they wore the same T-shirts.

Nancy loved this drink. She grinned at her reflection in the disco-mirrored backsplash. This had to be a kind of offical white-trash speedball, this late morning mixture of caffeine and alcohol, all she could afford on a small-town reporter's salary.

A joke, but the tingle gave her some guts. No, she told George, she was sure it was he who'd been seen at the Rosens', mere hours before the old guy went missing. Why even deny it? Honest work is honest work, and it was healthier doing construction than working in a bar.

As Darren returned to his proper place behind the bar once more, George's eyes widened, as if to plead with her, *Stop asking these stupid questions. He will fire me.*

So she asked a different kind of question—as in, "Surely you must have a social security card, since you're working here?" She waited for him to catch his breath, as she knew he'd had to, then dropped her smartphone onto the hard black surface of the bar.

She picked it up and made a show of scrolling through her hundreds of contact numbers. "See this one here? My local source at Homeland Security. I just have to lightly brush it here to tell him I'm having a great little drink with an illegal in a gay bar."

She turned the phone to show him the number. She pointed at it with her index finger, moving it slowly toward the shiny glass of the phone.

He whispered, "Wait. Don't call him, please, don't call him. Wait. I find the guy for you, the person who maybe knows something about Mr. Rosen. Who saw Mr. Rosen the day he disappeared. But it wasn't me. But I'll check."

Along with a two-buck tip, Nancy slid her business card across the bar.

■ ■ ■

"Don't worry about that bitch."

This was the second time Connor Hurst had said that about Nancy Argento. George and Connor were in a Greco & Greco truck on the way to a jobsite out in La Quinta. The monsoon wind that sometimes blew through this area in August had kicked in; the rotten-egg stench coming off the Salton Sea was inescapable, even with the doors sealed and the AC on high.

"I should tell you something—"

Connor turned into the driveway of the vacant house. "When we're done, OK? We're already late," he said. "George—you worry too much, man."

The front part of this house was a skeleton, already ripped down to the studs, the wiring and old plumbing. Two separate wings spread across the desert sand. George did the mental math and figured each side of the house was big enough to hold three, maybe four of the kind of trailer Alma, Jesse and Chuy Gomez lived in down in Mecca.

Maybe Connor was right, that Nancy had nothing to go on, she was guessing and hoping something would stick, or she'd scare George into telling her what had happened, into pointing the finger at the Indian tribe. But unless Jacy had blabbed about old Mr. Rosen, Connor still didn't know about the "accident."

Sy Greco met them at the door. The tall man did not look happy. Staring at Connor, he pointed at the sparkly Rolex on his wrist.

"I know, it was bumper-to-bumper on the 111," Connor said. "We got here as soon as we could."

Which was such a good lie, George thought. It was an easy traffic day if there ever was one. He was amazed Connor didn't miss a beat, didn't even blink.

"You should've left earlier, then," Sy said. "That's what I pay you for."

George looked at his boyfriend. Connor's mouth hung open for an instant, as if he was going to argue with Sy; then he changed his mind. Instead: "Boys out back?"

Sy nodded and Connor was off, disappearing into the partially destroyed structure. There was muffled laughter out there, no doubt Jacy and his cousin Paco, Hector, Ernesto, perhaps the two black guys from Indio, Rodney and Dante.

George didn't like being alone with Sy, though he was a rich, handsome, white American man who might be helpful in so many ways, even more than Connor. Also, being out back with the others he could keep his eye on Jacy.

Sy led him into the kitchen, not quite as gutted as the rest of the house. The sink was still there and so was the ceiling.

"What's your name again?" Sy asked, his hand on George's shoulder.

"George, George Gomes, *sir.*"

Sy tossed his phone onto a remaining counter, sending up a little puff of dust. "Can you remember? New counters, granite. New cabinets, maybe

Lucite. I don't know, let my wife tell you. New floor, of course. Write this down, George."

He handed George a pen and a clipboard with yellow paper on it. Sy looked up at the ceiling, and George did the same. Just like the Rosens' bathroom, old gray tiles ruined with age and water damage. "Fluorescents, Jesus Christ! Come here, let me show you something."

George moved closer to Sy, who stood behind him and put his big hands on the shorter man's shoulders, digging his fingers in. "See those lights up there? I'd like you to replace them."

George took in the dirty fluorescent strip begging to be dislodged. He wasn't surprised in the least that he felt Sy's heat from behind, then his breath on his neck.

He giggled—like he had when Jacy danced on Harry Rosen's grave— not stopping when he felt Sy's wet tongue on his neck, his arm around his chest, and his crotch pushed up against George's ass.

Uno, dos, tres, cuatro, cinco . . . there was a limit to how long he could stand this, though playing along would be part of the plan—as if this was as normal an activity as changing out the countertops or living in a vacant mansion or burying an old man under the sand. So in that entrepreneurial spirit, he pushed his ass back toward Sy.

"Señor Sy," he gasped, but the man's grip tightened, forcing the air out of George's lungs.

"I'm the boss here, remember that, George."

Heaven sent footsteps, getting louder by the second, on the floors, which had had all their carpets removed. George managed to wriggle free and choke out "Connor!" seconds before he reentered the kitchen.

■ ■ ■

Connor figured George would need some TLC, especially after this run-in with Sy. Their boss was a horny old goat and sooner or later hit on most everyone who worked for him, so he'd known it was only a matter of time for George.

And who could blame him—those big brown eyes, that smooth cinnamon-colored skin, the light dusting of fine black hair in all the right places. His quiet voice, the small stature that invited protection, invited adoration. Even now, his head turned to the truck window, the breeze making a mess of that jet-black hair.

They snaked their way up Highway 62 from the Coachella Valley floor, through the sunburned canyon formed by millions of years of earthquakes, on their way to Vi Gamble's place on Anaconda Lane in Yucca Valley.

Connor had some cash to deliver to little brother Locker for his garage business venture. Vi would make dinner, and though he'd never admit to wanting his mother to meet George, he was curious what her reaction would be to his new Mexican "friend."

These wistful visions of Mom's macaroni ended when the beautiful George Gomes turned his head back to Connor and began an unbelievable tale about Jacy Martin and an old fart they both worked with.

He got worked up; his voice got higher and squeakier until he sounded like a little Spanish high school girl who ends every sentence as a question. Then the tears started.

There'd been an accident at the grocery store, or outside of it. A shouting match; right, that little troublemaker Jacy did have a short fuse. Everybody knew that and no one took him seriously, come on.

So they ended up doing the stupidest thing they could dream up. Every minute they had argued about taking the old guy to a hospital sealed his particularly awful end. And with it, new problems for all of them.

They buried Harry Rosen somewhere out there in the valley sand. All George knew about the location was that he could see the lights of desert cities in the distance, but he wouldn't know how to ever find it.

Not much help there.

Where Connor Hurst could be of help was in consolation mode. Consolation and protection. Steering with one hand was difficult because of the twists in the canyon road, but he was able to rub George's thigh and to assure him it would all be OK.

It would be OK because they'd never tell anyone, never speak about it again, and really, the cops in this town did not have the resources to figure this one out.

Connor asked George if he could try and forget about it. Basically, just forget it. See how that would fly. He wouldn't have to return to do any work for the Rosens; neither would Jacy. How nuts would that be?

George gave him a look that suggested ever forgetting what they did would be impossible. But sharing the news seemed to work a little; at least the kid stopped bawling.

They pulled over a block away from Vi's so George could get it together, blow his nose, comb his hair. Where he'd seemed moments ago to be so distraught, now he was even giggling and wondering what kind of food "your mama make for me?"

■ ■ ■

It was a Tuesday; what did she warm up that day? Connor's mother was nothing if not predictable, or she tried to be. Likely there'd be chicken, fried; likely there'd be potatoes, mashed. She made the same thing at least three days out of the week, summer or winter, so it wasn't too much of a stretch to give George realistic menu options.

She'd be in a good mood and pretend to be happy, he figured, if all three sons—Connor, Locker, Duane—were at the table at once, now a rarity since Connor lived in that rich man's house, or more accurately, in that rich man's casita out back, while banging both him and his wife on different days, or at different times even on the same day.

George was quiet the last couple of blocks to the house. He'd stopped crying, those big brown eyes now dry, a little pink around the rims. He hardly seemed like the kind of man who could kill another and then cover it up. He seemed more like a contented pup, face pressed against the cool passenger window, watching the desert's dry scenery roll past.

Vi Gamble did not disappoint. Connor picked up the fry and spice aroma before he opened her front door. He grabbed one of the mints she kept in that ugly candy dish, popping another into George's mouth.

He shot Connor that smile that both melted his heart and hardened his cock. Given a little time and enough busyness, they'd both forget the unfortunate Rosen episode and go on as before.

Keep telling yourself, it was only a dream, it's not like it really happened. You said yourself, George Gomes, you couldn't find the spot again, you didn't know where it was. When the temperatures go up in the summer, people have nightmares. It's a fact.

Of the three brothers, Locker was the least likely to ever attend to anything that might be construed as a typical family detail—like his mother's chicken dinners. Yet there he was, wearing salmon-colored chinos and loafers with no socks, sitting at her table, like a refugee from a *GQ* photo shoot stranded in the boonies.

Duane was also present, no surprise there. Not a beneficiary of the Hurst height, more on a par with George, who sat across from him. Talk about opposites: George—black hair, dark skin, dark eyes, pleasant and open. Duane—blond, fair and covered in ink, blue eyes, moody, secretive.

For a long time Connor felt bad that he got along with Locker but not with Duane. He was only a half brother, so maybe that was it, something in the blood that just didn't mix. One day he just shrugged it off forever, and Duane became this person connected to his mother he'd try to get on with.

Connor introduced George Gomes to them as a coworker at Greco & Greco. He wondered whether Duane's stink eye was because George was a Mex or because George was having sex with Connor or because little half brother was a dope fiend.

Vi placed a chipped orange bowl filled with mashed potatoes in front of Connor, whispering, "This one's cute. You doing him?" loud enough for everyone to hear, including George.

Locker covered his mouth and turned away, trying not to spit on his shirt, his pretty shirt. Polka dots—where did he find shit like this?

Duane had to pretend he didn't hear. He tucked into the chicken, then the mashed. Then he got up, no explanation, no excuse, and left the room. Still chewing. A slammed door down the hall, the room Connor never went in.

George threw him a look. The slightest shrug, secret communication with the eyes, intended for him only but easily read by Vi and by Locker.

"He's skimming, you know," Connor said, turning to Vi. "Duane."

"Shut up. Shut up and eat. Don't you come into my house and lie."

Locker had brought a jar of peanut butter to the table. He ignored Vi's dinner and instead dug spoonfuls right out of the jar. "He's right. Bro's stealing, Mom," he said. "It's not just the twins saying so."

Locker's measured coolness threw her. Of all her sons, Connor knew he was the one she trusted, or trusted most. She'd listen to him.

Still, she said, "Duane would never steal from me."

Oh, yes, he would. And so would we.

Funny thing, Vi Gamble was a better cook than she was a dope dealer, but the food wasn't all that good; the chicken was dry, and Connor never really liked potatoes.

"Let's shoot something out back," Connor said, his hand sliding under the table to squeeze George's thigh. "I need some target practice."

■ ■ ■

While they were shooting into the hill that backed up onto Vi's rear yard, a hill devoid of almost all interest other than the prickly pear and other dusty desert scrub, Connor suggested to Locker it was dudes like George and some of the rest of the Greco & Greco crew who could help him open up Locker's Garage, get it ready when the time came.

A lot of these guys could fix a broken machine—which, let's face it, was really all a car was—as easily as they could drywall or paint.

Locker bought into the idea, thanked his brother. George stood off to the side with that smile he had, the one that had forgotten, temporarily, about Harry Rosen and Sy.

Connor would never have guessed in a million years that George knew how to shoot the Glock pistol Locker kept and was also familiar with the shotgun Vi had by the back door; in fact, George hit more bottles more times than both Connor and Locker together.

■ ■ ■

Connor kept Pilar waiting, something about traffic coming down the hill from Morongo. Rush hour, such as it was in Palm Springs. It was a real thing; still, the longer he delayed their "meeting," the closer it would be to when Sy inevitably returned here, to his own house, to his own home.

During their sex, the floor-to-ceiling gauzy mauve panel she'd installed over the French patio doors rustled; odd to have a breeze in August, particularly from this direction. She kept thinking it might be Sy—or worse, one of the workers, or even Marina, their maid. Even though she knew it wasn't any one of them, this was a game Pilar liked to play.

His thrusting against her was rough and routine, unusual for Connor, who was normally so thoughtful. Had she seen an article that addressed this precise issue—"What to Do When Sex with Your Pool Boy Gets Boring"—or had she just conjured this up out of the ether? It didn't matter, since she had no solution to the immediate problem.

Marina hadn't cleaned the room yet today. Even more likely she'd knock in her clipped, European habit and not wait for an answer before entering. Pilar shuddered. Which Connor took as a response to his skills as a lover.

So be it; let him think that. It would be helpful for them both, in the long con. Connor hadn't said anything about the Wellbutrin on the same dresser top as the photo of Angel Greco at age eleven, this one taken at dusk during the town's weekly street fair. One of her favorites: a son indulging his shutterbug mom.

Connor had asked about it once, asked why she kept it around. "Doesn't this depress you?" he asked, trying to be helpful, not realizing the photo was for her the most precious object in the room.

It didn't make her depressed. It made her hopeful. Pilar Greco was not embarrassed that her dead child's image watched her make love with someone other than his father. If he was still alive she might've thought differently.

Angel would have liked Connor, she realized. He was like a fun uncle, perhaps, though different from his father. Let him get away with some things, less strict.

Connor collapsed on top of her. *OK, that's done,* she thought.

His hot breath, quick at first, drew out. "I think Sy knows," he whispered.

Muffled bumps in the direction of the hallway, an inch or two of board between their naked bodies and whoever was there—Marina, one of the workers, Candy even; it could be that damn dog. It could be Sy and then he *would* know.

"Why do you say that? He doesn't know anything—"

"The way he looks at me. Got a feeling that somebody like Jimbo, or that jackass Jacy, said something. They don't like me being the boss when Sy's not around."

Would Angel have said something like *Chill, dude?* He would've been a teenager by now; he would have become her enemy.

"He doesn't know and he doesn't care. Sy's only concern is Sy."

Connor was off her now, on his back, staring at the ceiling, quiet.

Pilar sat up, catching her reflection in the mirror. Normally she'd put on her robe, but it was such a hot day, even with the air-conditioning, the enveloping desert relentless. And—truth was, she looked good; she looked damn fine naked for a woman a couple of years away from fifty. If not exactly perky, her breasts still had nipples that pointed out, if not up. She'd never had a big chest and resisted all the thoughts about augmentation, and she was proud of that.

So she'd leave the robe off, make him happy—she supposed it would: *MILF crosses languidly from bed to bar to offer sweaty, spent lover refreshment.*

There was a new treasure here, if Sy hadn't removed it. "I need a little something," she said. "Here it is—Black Maple Hill. Sy says it costs two hundred dollars a pop." She turned, holding the bottle up.

"God. I hate that shit," Connor said. "If I drink in the afternoon I'll get a headache."

"I'm going to have one." She poured herself a small amount, a thimbleful. Angel watched as she downed it. He probably didn't approve. She wouldn't look at his photo again today.

"And another." Nothing like a little bourbon to make the recent bad sex less disappointing. "I asked Sy for a divorce."

Connor turned to face her and sat up in the bed. He laughed.

"He said no."

"You're kidding me, right? You didn't ask him for a divorce."

"But I wanted to."

Struck with sudden ridiculous modesty, Pilar covered her right breast with her left hand and walked her drink back to the bed. "There's other things in the bar, if you want something."

He ran his fingers down the ridges of her spine, making her shiver.

"He'll be gone soon enough."

"Let's go over it one more time."

Connor turned away, toward the fully covered window. "God, do we have to?"

Now that she'd segued into leading a meeting, attire was appropriate. Pilar wrapped her pink summer robe around her shoulders, tying it under her breasts.

"You're not going to get his money if he's not dead, now, are you?"

Connor stared through the curtain and the glass, out to where the pool was.

"Sy has a little drink every night around midnight," he said.

She sat down next to him. "That's right; he sips it. Unlike me."

"Even so, he's always asleep by twelve thirty. Out like a light."

"Always." She pulled his chin to the right so she could look him in the eye. "We're still in on this?"

Connor nodded.

She rose and walked back to the bar, pulling open the hidden door to a small storage area under the counter. "He keeps the bottle down here. I'll make sure the Xanax—all of it—is dissolved in here before I head down to Laguna."

He was looking at her, yet he wasn't seeing her. This new distance she picked up on was troublesome. He couldn't be equivocal with this; getting rid of Sy would work only if they were both all in.

"Don't scare me, Connor." She was back on the bed, his hand gently pulling the robe off her shoulder.

"I just want to make sure that's enough of the drug to knock the bastard out. You have the dose figured?"

■ ■ ■

Jacy Martin was by nature a nervous individual, and when he went more than a couple of hours without seeing or hearing his love, Kaya Belardo, the stress *blew him up.* Like that big-ass mountain outside, Jacinto, his namesake, a giant thrust escarpment that exploded out of the desert floor—the same thing could happen to him.

It did and it had, recently. In the timeless cool of Montana Grande Casino, a short little Indian in a ridiculous purple costume that made him look like a circus monkey didn't seem like much of a threat to anybody.

This was his secret. *Take a good look, all you fat old white men with your money and your ugly wives! Be cool, or you too might find yourself under a couple of tons of sand like that loud prick Harry Rosen.*

Where was Kaya? She had a shift today, he was certain. She avoided him when his dark moods took over. Maybe this was one of those times. She was with Andreas; he liked her around; he would find things to keep her in the back offices.

While Andreas watched him the entire time through the casino floor cameras. Of that he was certain. Even now, he zeroed in on a camera on a wall to his right, careful not to move his head to give himself away. He looked right into the lens, like he could see directly into the dark heart of Andreas Alvarado.

Then there was something else to distract him. The casino patrons, the dying white men and their horrible wives—as well as his fellow employees, the dealers, cashiers, security—were directing their attention toward the front of the casino, the doorway itself.

So Jacy Martin felt sick, like he would puke up his breakfast right there on the casino carpet, when he saw what everyone was looking at: a woman dressed all in black, complete with black hat and black veil, like it was Halloween, like a Halloween witch. He felt sick because he knew who this was and he knew why she was dressed this way.

He'd heard that Carole Blair Rosen had been a movie star or something. These people had a flair for the dramatic, even if no one knew who they were anymore. But she wouldn't be the star in this casino.

He got in front of her. "Ma'am," he said, "can I help you?"

Carole kept walking. She was headed toward the offices in back, toward Andreas Alvarado.

"Ma'am! Where you going?"

So softly he could hardly hear, she said, "I'd like to see Mr. Manager from your tribe."

Jacy put his hand on her forearm. "Sorry, miss, he's out today."

Carole wrenched her arm away from the little man. "Harry! My Harry's missing!" she screamed.

6

Jacy tried hard to imagine that his young love, Kaya Belardo, would some-day be as old as Carole Blair Rosen.

This white woman was so loud, and so full of complaining, and so intent on drawing attention to her side while simultaneously sucking all other living spirit right out of the room.

Which happened to be the casino office of Andreas Alvarado. Jacy's least favorite place.

Kaya might become old someday—as surely they both would—as rich and respected members of their tribe. But she wouldn't be like this. His lady was soft-spoken. She was dignified, as befitted the future mother of his children.

The way Carole's head, topped with that little square black hat and the long black veil that fell from it, swayed from side to side made him dizzy. Andreas insisted Jacy sit behind her, near the office door, main goon Mike standing next to him, leaning against the wall with his arms folded over his huge chest.

Mike—one of the two assholes who'd held Jacy upside down and shook him, like a fucking saltshaker, the last time he was in this office, humiliating him.

You just wait, Andreas. I'll get you and I'll get your men, too. You just wait.

He didn't even want to acknowledge that Kaya, indeed, was in the room. She was. Standing right to the side of Andreas's desk, a perfectly sweet sergeant at arms. Their eyes would not meet. If they did, he knew Andreas would see; he would know this, no matter what it was he was involved in.

Andreas was in a project to calm Carole Rosen. He would try anything, but he'd start with alcohol.

She sat in her black in her chair with a fruity, old-lady cocktail that made use of the casino's totem pole swizzle sticks—totally the wrong tribe, but the white people never noticed that. That was her right hand. Her left held an unlit cig in the stupid skinny holder she carried.

He followed the drink as it spun around, and then the old whore was staring right at him, her cunt drunk-bitch eyes on fire.

"It was him! This *boy* in the silly purple jacket here. *I'm sure* he's the one I saw in Ralph's, talking to Harry." She took a sip and turned back to the boss.

Andreas paused before speaking. Jacy knew he wasn't all that smart—so Andreas had this little move where he clasped his hands in front of his mouth. Like Solomon from the Bible, about to pass judgment.

"Now, Mrs. Blair—"

"Rosen. I haven't been Carole Blair since 1966."

Andreas's eyes opened wide. "It was dark, right? Mrs. *Rosen?* Probably someone else you saw." Then he smiled, the fucker smiled, and in Jacy's direction. "This boy here spends his whole life working for *me* in the casino." The fatso chuckled.

"It wasn't dark; it was twilight—and it was inside the store. They had all their lights on." She pulled a silver lighter out of the little black bag dangling from her wrist. "May I light up?"

Outside the office walls a cheer went up. Muffled bells, high-pitched screeches from winners, even whistling. Jacy turned his head to look through the one-way mirror; a small crowd gathered around one of the craps tables.

"I don't allow smoking in my office."

"I thought you were your own damn country," Carole said. "I'm so upset; I really am. Not only is my Harry missing; we can't pay these bills you've been sending out for the remodel. He's sure you and the Grecos are overcharging."

At last, Jacy's eyes met Kaya's. She looked down at the floor, covered in the same crazy-pattern carpet Montana Grande used in the casino itself. Carole tossed her unlit cigarette onto the rug, where it rolled under Andreas's desk.

He pulled open his desk drawer—where he kept pens and Post-its, certainly, but also his whiskey and one or more guns. "Have you gone to the police about your husband?" he asked.

"I don't think you're listening to me."

"We are, ma'am, of course we are," Kaya said, breaking her silence. She put her hand on Carole's shoulder. The older woman stiffened.

Andreas tossed what Jacy recognized as the casino's bright activity coupons onto his desk, deals for senior dining and keno games, all those things that kept old bags like Carole coming through the doors. He topped this little pile off with a tribe-branded visor in their signature colors of blue and orange.

He was going to try to buy her off with this shit. "What do the police say, Mrs. Rosen?" Andreas asked.

She sucked on her empty cigarette holder as if it were lit with something. "I went down there; I filled in the missing persons report for my husband. Honestly, they were so terribly condescending to me," she said. "They think he's dead and I'm just a foolish old woman. I hate the cops in this town."

"Now, you're not, don't say that, honey." Kaya did her best to appear concerned. She scooped up the promos and handed them to Carole, finishing with a quick and tentative little rub on the arm.

"We've got some good connections down there. I'll make a couple of calls," Andreas said.

Jacy dug his fingers into the chair's armrests to keep from bouncing off the ceiling. *Some connections, right, Andreas!* He knew his boss wouldn't set foot within a mile of the Palm Springs cop shop. It was a gigantic mutual hatred society.

Carole opened her little black bag. She pulled out several pill bottles: "He's an old man. I have the blood pressure, the diabetes, the angina, the Razadyne, all his medicine, all right here in this bag. He needs to get it right away."

Then she started crying again, and sniffling, and there were these awful old-lady secretions and liquids coming off her face. Jacy turned his head to the wall while Kaya held out a box of tissues.

■ ■ ■

Most folks don't realize the most disgusting material you can imagine gets stuck to the casters welded onto big commercial Dumpsters.

But Jacy Martin knew. Jacy Martin got this ant's-eye view again, out back of the casino, courtesy of Andreas's guy Mike. Who was strong enough to hold him up by himself. And to do the ankle shake, that old shakedown.

Jacy's forearms crossed over his forehead, making a little cushion, because he didn't trust this big goon. His grip might slip and crash the poor little Indian brave onto the dirty, greasy concrete, headfirst.

Andreas screamed, "You killed that old man, didn't you, you fucking idiot!" His hard-soled foot landed in Jacy's armpit, the cry of pain drowned out only by the dusk wind howling down out of the north.

"Boss, boss, stop it! Stop it, please, man, *please*! It was an accident, I swear to you, nobody meant no harm to that Mr. Rosen."

A delivery truck, their linen service, their white tablecloth *angel*, came into his field of vision. He knew the guy would back into the space where they were playing this out. He'd need to unload Montana Grande's order.

Andreas grabbed Mike's arm. "Put him down. Slowly," he said.

Jacy curled himself into a little ball as he was lowered onto the pavement. He seemed OK; nothing was bleeding. Yet. "It was a mistake, Andreas. We had to get rid of the body."

"*We?* What the fuck, *mijo*? What do you mean, *we?*"

Jacy had to shout over the truck's back-up alarm. If he didn't move in another ten seconds this truck would crush him. "This Mexican fag kid George was with me—he did it. He did it! I had to cover up for him, like usual," he said, rolling over to the right, out of the way of the linen truck.

Mike and Andreas stood there like fools, like they were waiting for this delivery, and little old Jacy was nothing more than a lump of disgusting dirty laundry lying against the curb.

He stood up and brushed himself off. "I was saving our good names, cousin Andreas," he said. "That's what I always do for you."

■ ■ ■

Kaya Belardo watched as Andreas lay there staring at the ceiling from his bed, though he seemed to look beyond it, like he could maybe see through the roof to the stars or something. Perhaps he saw the future, as he was the tribe's leader; maybe he had that foresight power.

Many of their people had that odd way about them in the old days, or so she'd been told, though now so much was forgotten. Could he see right through her? Kaya wondered about that, worried Andreas might be reading her thoughts *at this very moment*. But then, he wasn't the type to keep something like that in, either.

Magdalene, help me. Didn't she also have to play second fiddle to all those fucking apostles, all twelve of those men, when she was really the smartest of the bunch?

Kaya sat on top of him. He was such a large man, if she had to have sex with Andreas, this was the easiest way to do it, especially as short as she was. Also, being above him gave the illusion that it—this sham of a relationship—was under her control.

Though she knew it wasn't. It wasn't now and it would never be so, not until they—she and Jacy—finally left the res and Andreas and Palm Springs far behind them.

But tonight there was a problem. "I feel so sorry for Jacy," she said, hoping it didn't come out too much like a question, almost a whisper, this kind of post-sex conversation she and Andreas had from time to time.

He grunted. "He fucked up big time. There's consequences."

Kaya put her hands on his chest, rubbing him across his fleshy breast. Maybe the fire she made with massage would sink deep into his cold heart.

"We come up, he and me, together at the Guadalupe School, all eight years—"

"You will do as I say, and watch him for me, Kaya. "

■ ■ ■

Vi Gamble sometimes worried that she watched too much TV. Though Greg Hurst—Connor and Locker's father—was a bum on most counts, he didn't like his family spending much time in front of the tube, and would often walk in front of the screen, turn it off and stand there facing them with his arms folded over his chest.

Invariably this would be followed by a hellish couple of hours outside in the sun and dirt and dead grass with the two toddlers, watching them try to kill each other.

Though Mr. Hurst left shortly after that and hadn't been back since, she must've internalized his idiot-box admonitions. OK, so she'd get up in a minute. She was now an old lady—well, maybe not exactly old, but certainly older than everyone around her.

If she thought about him too much, she'd seethe. Same thing with the other ex, Teddy Gamble, who also left her to be daddy as well as mommy to not only two but now three boys. She lit up another cigarette.

The truth was Vi liked watching the reality shows. They often featured the kind of man she went for, a little (or a lot) rough around the edges, the kind of man who'd been redeemed and could make things with his own hands. The kind of man who was an *artisan*.

In a way, what she and the boys did on Anaconda Lane in Yucca Valley was artisanal. A home-based business; they worked with their hands inasmuch as they took cash and counted and bundled it and they bagged up product and stacked and hid it when they didn't sell it. She could be proud of being a small business owner, especially now as the economy crumbled around her.

All this was reflected in reality TV: entrepreneurship, reinvention (especially of baby boomers, of which Vi Gamble was a card-carrying example), usually starring men of the kind she could find in any local high-desert hardware store.

Like the one who was on the TV right now. He was a picker, a guy who went from flea market to garage sale to back alley looking for cast-off treasures he would then sell online or to retail antique dealers.

"The most important thing is finding items people are willing to pay top dollar for," he said. "Otherwise, there's not much joy here."

There's not much joy here. It was like he was speaking directly to Vi, referencing her dwindling drug business.

A jarring interruption (like the appearance of an unwanted thunderhead at a picnic), Duane Gamble entered, flopped onto the recliner and pushed it back. This type of job might be something he could do if they weren't already selling dope—this "picking" thing—though the guy on the TV had more energy than Duane would likely muster up in three lifetimes.

Vi watched him out of the corner of her eye as he lit a cigarette. Impossible; the ambition required for this leap was just not there. She doubted it would ever be.

"What you looking at, Ma?"

The sun was going down; he already had or soon would have one of his guns in his pocket, a habit of his even she was now used to. Afraid of the dark, *you know*, and anyone could come to the door, come busting in, *right?*

"You stealing from me, son?"

There, she'd said it. There'd be no turning back; it was like lighting a fuse to a bomb.

Duane didn't look angry, at least not right away. He looked confused. Maybe betrayed. The realization sank in over his features, a slow wave. *This is what happens when you drop out of high school as a sophomore: too dumb to process the information.*

He shifted in the recliner, skinny little ass hitting the chair frame on the right. The picker on the TV insisted to a moist housewife with a

Mitteleuropean-looking tchotchke that "this isn't the real thing, this is a fake, and we don't buy fakes here."

Vi was banking on the notion that Connor was right, that Duane was skimming on sales, even if he hadn't provided much evidence. She could trust number one son; they were in this deal together. He'd said both Marines, those twins Timbo and Jimbo, confirmed it. *They saw it. They saw you, Duane, taking money and drugs. From* me. *Your mother. From us. Your family. Why, Duane,* why?

Duane Gamble was a cornered dog, his tatted arms pressed to the faux leather, hands gripping the armrests. His blue eyes (from her) darted from Vi to the TV and back, frantic for an object to land and focus on.

"Connor lies to you," he said. "Call the Marines; call them now! Let's talk to them."

He fished his phone out of his back pocket. Duane threw it at her from across the room. It sailed past the TV guy with his embarrassed guest, landing on the floor next to Vi's leg.

She picked it up, but the truth was she didn't know how to work this thing. "You call them; I'll talk to them," she said, tossing the phone back at Duane and hitting him in the stomach.

"He's making it all up, Ma; he's trying to make me look bad." He punched in a code on his phone. She heard it ring on the other end. It sounded like voice mail picked up; it was one of the twins, she was sure.

"Call me, Jimbo. It's important," Duane said, ending the call.

He dropped the phone on the table next to the recliner, nodding to the TV. "I guess we'll see what he says when he calls back. Right?"

She wondered why he'd make that call when it was so obvious Duane would be found out as the idiot liar he was. Unless she was wrong about the whole business. Unless her other sons weren't as honest as she'd always believed them to be.

"Connor is with Locker, Ma. They don't want me around 'cause I'll tell the truth. It's them stealing. If there's any stealing going on, it's all for Locker's dumb idea to have a car repair business. Can't you see that?"

Vi Gamble was the type of woman who stuck to an idea once she had it in her head and she didn't like to be challenged on it. But what if Duane was right?

Locker had asked for money and she'd laughed at him. Not because his idea was stupid, but because she didn't have it and he should've known better.

And Connor—well, yes. All of their futures depended on his thing going on down there in Palm Springs. She needed it to happen. Why would he ever lie to her?

■ ■ ■

Sy Greco had so many things to be proud of. One of the key places, though, where it all came together and he could gaze upon it—if that wasn't too ridiculous a way to think about it, and it wasn't, no, it wasn't; he deserved his success—was the summer fund-raising gala for the City Film Festival.

He'd been asked to serve on the steering committee two years before and he took the task to heart. He opened up his envied Rolodex to the board, thus allowing them to beg for money from his acquaintances. Even he realized it would be a stretch to consider them friends, though perhaps there were a few who still fit that description.

Sy and Pilar Greco were fine examples of civic boosters. Everyone knew them; everyone knew the Greco team was improving historic Palm Springs housing stock by their remodels and spectacular sales. In the process, everyone got lifted up; everyone's life improved. In fact, they could crown him honorary mayor right now. This would be the perfect occasion.

For the event they'd taken over the greens at the O'Donnell Golf Course, shoved up against Mount San Jacinto, and adjacent to the town's toniest neighborhood at Old Las Palmas. The little old rich ladies wouldn't have to drive far to part with their money and wouldn't have to worry about the relentless sun, which made its daily exit over the giant mountain to the west well before dusk.

Sy's influence had yet to extend to the decor committee. Like so many desert events, this one was over-the-top with the white drapery everywhere. He thought it was likely a rich women's collective idea of heaven, all billowy, cloudlike shapes set against the muted greens of the course. The kind of thing Pilar would love.

Not that Sy had any real idea for an alternative; heaven was where son Angel resided and that kind of lady-peaceful environment was the last thing a twelve-year-old boy wanted or needed. Fuck it. He didn't have to think about it; he wouldn't think about it and make his own black clouds descend. Instead, he took another big gulp of the champagne he'd been given when he arrived.

Maybe it was correct that he wasn't so much a latent "homosexual" as a desperate man fleeing the mother of his child just because her every expression reminded him of their son. Though, truly, his breaking old heart still skipped a beat whenever Connor Hurst entered a room.

And now here was that hot Jorge kid who called himself George. Right here at this party. Help, of course, but looking as cute as anything in the pastel blue polo they made him wear over tight black khakis. He served little bites from a silver tray nearly as large as he was.

Their eyes connected but George looked away. Sy didn't especially like his employees moonlighting, but they all did it; they all had to since the Greco remodels were sporadic. No, he suspected George's shyness was more of a personal tic, embarrassed because of his recent attentions at the work site. Sy would have him, eventually; this was inevitable, and George would be better served to simply accept this.

He'd insist in the future that his boys wear better-fitting clothing. All of them, but especially the Latin guys, wore light-colored loose pants and shirts, as was the desert custom. Sy, for one, wanted to see more flesh.

George and his tray walked by pretending to ignore, and the view was just as nice—if not nicer—from the back. He stopped at a little group that included the mayor, who noticed Sy and moved toward him.

Please, not this clown. Palm Springs mayor, Alan Franz, was a little bit chunky and used a harsh chemical treatment to keep his thin hair the "red" he'd been born with, or so he must've thought. The overall effect was rather orange, still-hanging-on-the-tree orange, and today the good mayor had a spray-on tan to match.

"Don't you turn away from me, Sy Greco. I see you there," he said. Franz stuffed the little canapé he'd grabbed from George's tray into his mouth.

"Mr. Mayor." Sy raised his glass an inch in a perfunctory toast.

"Since our senior gals make up about forty percent of the electorate," Franz said, while chewing, "I try not to irritate them."

Sy wanted to look at anything but this man's open mouth, bits of toasted bread stuck between his teeth. "And you're telling me this—"

"Because Brenda the Bride moved into my fucking office; that's why."

Sy was confused and was only on his first drink.

"Carole Blair, now Carole Rosen, comes in and she says Greco's doing some work over there."

Small, ad hoc groups of cocktail party chatterers closed in as the lawn filled. For sure, someone would be listening. Sy lowered his voice.

"*Brenda the Bride.* I didn't think anybody remembered that turkey."

Mayor Franz inhaled the rest of his appetizer. "I'm as old as you are. The point being, she has complaints about the Greco work; she demands to see the city attorney—"

"That's got to gall you, Alan. One more Alzheimer's patient off her meds, ruining your day." Sy could swear the singer being piped in over their heads was Rosemary Clooney, "Mambo Italiano," outrageously dated, even for this crowd.

Alan Franz scooped yet another cheesy hors d'oeuvre off a passing tray, this one wielded by someone not on the Greco payroll. He pushed it into Sy's chest, making him take a step back. "I'd ignore her, Sy Greco, but strangely, the PS police get a similar story from an old lady in a wheelchair, homeless now, no less—who tells us you're *Satan.*"

Sy brushed the crumbs off his tan linen jacket. "Let me tell you something. Some women don't plan for their future. *At all.* Then old reliable croaks—and it's like a one-way ticket to hell. But it's not me—they do it to themselves."

Franz stood there chewing, staring at Sy, his next move not apparent. A big desert cockroach zigzagged across the patio toward them. Sy raised his foot and slammed his seven-hundred-dollar Prada loafer down on it.

"Pilar tells me Raid's toxic, so it's a good thing I've got these big feet," he said. "We're up on election year again. I've got some empty office space over on Tahquitz, maybe a good place for your staff, your volunteers? I know these campaigns don't come cheap. I'll make that price right."

■ ■ ■

Nancy Argento stood behind a pillar, not far from Mayor Franz and Sy Greco, listening, straining to hear what they said but picking up only a word here and there. Other than most of the help, she was likely the youngest person present. People would never guess a professional reporter would be paid as little as she was, yet hours earlier she'd found herself in a line at Sam's Payday Lender in Cathedral City picking up the cash for an appropriate outfit for this shindig.

She felt awkward in this summer dress. Her heroines had always been the types one would see on TV covering the Middle Eastern wars: strong women crouched in dung-walled bunkers wearing dirty khaki shorts, hiking boots, matching dusty flak jackets.

At least she was in a desert. That part was real, she thought, her attention diverted to the applause when a severely blond pianist on a raised platform eased into a Cole Porter tune. A good time for another sip of the ubiquitous champagne.

One can dream about the rest; this story has awards potential.

The mayor patted Sy on the arm, then moved away, nodding to a small group across the patio. An opening. Shy by nature—at least she had been, once, maybe— Nancy had trained herself to approach with a simple "one, two, three, go" technique.

By rote her feet moved toward him. Ernst had given her a teeth-bleaching gift certificate for her birthday. *Flash Greco that smile. Work it.*

He raised an eyebrow watching her advance, the last moments he would ever resemble anything close to arguably playful.

"I couldn't help but notice you there, Mr. Greco," she said.

He smiled. "I try to fade back into the scenery at this type of thing; that's not working tonight," he said, raising his glass.

She was happy he did that; she took another needed sip herself. "I don't believe we've met. Nancy Argento, *Desert Sun*."

If that surprised him, there was no way she could detect it. He either had a great poker face or her earlier questions about their company hadn't occupied much headroom with either Pilar or her husband.

"So you are," he said, shaking her hand. Respectful, professional, verging on the soporific. "You're new to Palm Springs."

She wasn't sure if he was stating the obvious or asking her. When in doubt—ask another question. "I'm so totally wrong on this, but did I just hear you trying to bribe our mayor?"

Sy laughed, nodding up to the arched covering hanging over them. "I'm sure whatever you thought you heard, my dear, was not that. These acoustics always play tricks. It's a fact."

She could feel her face warm up; this kind of shit always happened when she took the bait and had a drink at one of these things. The alcohol calmed her; it was necessary for breaking the ice. What other option was there?

"Whatever. That wasn't why I came. I'm here to see how the town supports the arts—the film festival—what the city values are, that sort of thing."

Nancy couldn't tell if he believed her or not. She was better at talking bullshit now than she'd been in Cleveland, for sure, but she still wasn't a master.

"You must know I'm on the board," he said. "Is that why you've been calling?"

So he *did* know her name, if not why she'd been contacting Greco & Greco. Progress.

"Funny, I was here to meet a guy to talk about your company, but right here in front me is what back in Ohio we'd call the real deal."

Now his brow was wrinkled. She'd gotten a reaction, however mild.

"A guy *here*? What guy here?"

Or maybe it was a big reaction. "What's wrong? Don't you like people talking to you about your company, about your very successful business?"

Sy paused for a difficult—at least to her—moment. "I'm always happy to answer questions about Greco—but I prefer to do it myself, not to have some *guy* put the words out there for me." He gestured with his now empty glass. "This party is full of my workers who moonlight. Palm Springs is like that; everybody's got a couple things going on."

Nancy relaxed a bit inside. Her stomach would not tear in half, but she could not believe she'd almost fucked up her first and possibly only chance to get something out of Sy Greco.

She might have memorized the list of questions left at her desk for the Greco interview, but she had not. She hadn't prepared well enough for this. That old veil of doubt—that her Cleveland bosses had been justified in firing her ass because, *let's face it*, she was a shitty reporter—descended and she looked down at her glass. "I need another drink," she said.

He laughed. "Don't we all. Look, Nancy, most people realize how generous I am once they get to know me—look around at this party, why don't you? Pilar and I love to support our little city. You'll understand that soon enough."

"Actually, what I'm trying to understand is why so many of the old folks you—as you put it—generously 'help' end up losing their homes, losing everything. Don't really see how that goes with 'generous' in any dictionary I've seen, but I guess that's the copy on your desk."

His face darkened once more, but she was on a roll and would not be yanked around. *Act as if, Nancy, act as if.*

"Ginny McCadden. Would she tell me about your stellar generosity?" Another waiter floated by with a tray full of champagne. She snatched one without even turning her head. "Or Carole Rosen—or more to the point, Harry Rosen, if anyone—"

"Wait," he commanded—not to her but to the help. "Give me one of those." He narrowed his eyes at Nancy, leaning in. She wondered if this big man would strike her, if she'd gone too far. "That woman is a drunk. She's dirty and lives under a bridge like an old troll. She fills this city with lies and I am sick and tired of those lies hurting my wife—and our business."

Hit her—no, of course not; they were at a public event. He did plant his hand on her upper arm, however, and squeeze. Hard.

She backed away. Sy didn't let go. "That hurts. Get your hand *off* me."

Like that, he released his grip. "Sorry, you got me going there." Then he laughed. "Here's what I suggest. Call me tomorrow; we'll have a little chat about our company where I can answer all your questions. But don't try to rely on crazy old women or my supposedly disgruntled employees. They'll steer you wrong every time."

Good! This unanticipated meeting in the future would give her the time to come up with a better game plan and questions. She was going to ask him what time was best when—

"Sweetheart, I simply can't let you have this gorgeous man all to yourself!" A pushy black woman dripping in jewelry (who'd obviously never heard the Chanel dictum "take one thing off") inserted herself between Nancy and Sy, lunging in to air-kiss him.

"Alice, you embarrass me. Every time. Do you know our *Desert Sun* reporter, Nancy—"

"Argento, Nancy Argento," she said, shaking the older woman's hand.

"This is Alice Jones, the chair of this little event here," he said.

"Hon, you don't mind if I steal Sy for a second? Shop talk," Alice said, and before Nancy could squeak out an answer, Alice hooked her arm into Sy's, pulling him out onto the green.

Well. *That was fast.* This time she would not beat herself up, come up with lines she should've, could've said, such as:

Wait your turn, bitch, we're talking.

Before you go, Sy, what time shall I call?

No, let's do it now. I'm writing the story for tomorrow on how you conspired to foreclose on seniors.

Where is Harry Rosen? I bet you know.

But she didn't get the chance because George was now in front of her, with his empty tray, smiling at her. He cocked his head. "You coming to work for Greco & Greco?"

Right, George. She trembled, a delayed reaction to the interruption she hadn't been prepared for. *And why not?* It's what Nancy, being a reporter, should have expected, even if this was, on the surface, a party.

"Maybe I will, George; maybe I will end up there. Who knows? Sometimes I wonder."

He was supposed to be working; instead, he fidgeted, passing his tray from right hand to left hand and back again, over and over.

"You're a busy guy. What is this, job number three? The Grecos, the bar, and now you're a party boy?"

"I work hard, always. You never know what might turn out to be the best job."

Indeed—a simple look around this Palm Springs crowd told her the ratio of rich men who'd want to "help" someone like George versus those who'd like her number was, well, off the charts.

She swallowed the last of her wine, wishing George could've been more helpful in that regard. "What are you doing with an empty tray? Your bosses won't like that."

He backed into the patio wall, into an indentation in the bougainvillea, though any discerning eye could see him idling there.

"I want to ask you not to tell on me, please, with the Homeland Security. I need to stay here. I found out who was with Señor Rosen that night—"

"Save your breath, George." She handed him the empty glass. "You're off the hook. Carole Rosen told me all about Jacy—*and you.*"

■ ■ ■

When a real lady checks her watch, it should lend an air of mystery to the persona she's created. Since nobody wore a watch much anymore, the action had double—no, triple—the effect.

Pilar Greco sat waiting for Nancy Argento in the aqua reception room of Vitaspring Spa. She checked her watch—a Cartier Sy had given her when she'd announced her pregnancy with Angel almost thirteen years earlier.

Just about ten A.M. The sunlight played with the gold band when she rotated her forearm. She wondered if the girls at the desk noticed, if they thought, like she did, that the pose and her style warranted a glossy magazine ad.

Pilar was grateful for even that momentary distraction. In a little more than twenty-four hours the plan she and Connor had concocted would turn her into a tragic widow. Even the thought of this might send her over the edge into panic; she'd keep it at the periphery of her consciousness, which was where this writer came in.

Where the fuck is Nancy Argento?

Sy had literally cornered Pilar at the film festival gala, insisting she meet with Nancy again. He was convinced that if she saw Pilar both as a friend and as a way to get good local contacts, the reporter would drop this "silly" fascination she had with local old people and their houses.

And Pilar could've killed Sy for making her go through with it! No matter. She smiled at her own dark little joke and heard the door open with a gush of hot desert wind.

Nancy, at last.

■ ■ ■

They—or rather Pilar, since the Grecos were paying the bill *and* it was their idea—signed up for one of Vitaspring's offerings for two ladies with too much money on any particular day.

Nancy and Pilar soaked together, inches apart, in the shaded mineral pools, which were supposed to relax them, though Pilar felt anything but rested. Maybe it had a delayed effect. Alcohol was not part of official spa-day protocol, but she could sure use a drink.

Nancy was enchanted by it all; Sy was right, throwing money at rubes like her could distract them. For a reporter, this one hadn't seemed too aggressive up to this point; yet Pilar always got the feeling that would change fast, without warning.

It was like that old TV show about the detective everybody thought was dumb; then he turned out to be the smartest one of the bunch. Maybe

Nancy was like that. Or maybe she just wasn't an award-winning reporter. Let's face it: The *Desert Sun* wasn't exactly the *Wall Street Journal*.

She'd find out. In fact, Pilar had hired Jacy Martin to hang out in the parking lot and keep an eye on Nancy once they were done with girl time.

Still, Pilar couldn't shake this odd feeling of protectiveness. That was what it had to be. Nancy was small, thin; Pilar hadn't realized what a great figure she had until they were in the pool together. Their thighs had touched a couple of times by accident—this would happen when you were in a whirlpool together. Honestly, Pilar was old enough to be Nancy's mother—if she had a mother on the younger, hotter side.

So it was this motherly feeling Pilar was channeling when out of the Jacuzzi gurgles and the light breeze in the palm fronds above came this: "So—should I tell you what I think is going on?"

"Going on?"

"Oh, come on, Pilar. I think you and your husband have found a fairly easy way to make a lot of money from this current obsession with mid-century homes. Lucky for you two, Palm Springs is full of them."

They were soon facedown on adjacent tables, each having a thick coating of dark clay brushed onto her back to deep cleanse, to detox. The two attendants applying the mud had an almost nunlike quality to their outfits—white frocks, white hats that covered all their hair, like helmets—nor did they seem to hear anything that was being said.

"We've been happy and lucky to ride that wave," Pilar said. "We were in the right place at the right time."

"Isn't it unethical for a realtor to offer those extensive home-remodeling services?"

Pilar's attendant laid a cool linen sheet on her back. They would both be wrapped up like mummies.

"Well, it's not that simple. That business—the remodeling outfit—is owned by the Indian tribe. I'm sure you know that. Sy helps them out; he's their executive presence."

"Seems like there's an awful lot of unhappy old ladies in town who never thought they'd be back in tiny apartments."

"It's not like anybody forced those people to have work done on their houses. That's unfortunate. It happens. If you can't pay—you can't pay."

One of the spectral attendants turned down the dimmers to the room, leaving them in afternoon darkness.

"Is this when we get the cucumber slices for our eyelids?" Nancy asked, an unbidden giggle escaping along with the question.

"You've been watching too much TV, I think," Pilar said. Her phone vibrated softly against her hip, where she'd stashed it despite the stern look of her attendant. She'd said an important call was expected. A lie, but you never knew, and ever since Angel, Pilar needed to be constantly available.

She was going to answer when: "Do you read the Bible, Pilar? I assume with your background you'd be Catholic; is that right? Didn't you ever read the part about usury?"

The call went unanswered, and she felt herself get not just warm, but hot. This clay mixture might be drawing out the poisons, but it did nothing to deter her anger.

"I stopped believing in God when he took my boy."

The room went quiet again. *So, that shut the bitch up.*

And the phone buzzed again, this insistence against her side. It must be important, maybe the same caller. Pilar fished it out of the linen and clay and saw it was their maid, Marina Boyko. She answered with a whisper.

"This better be—

"Oh, Miss Greco! You must come at once—it is Connor—"

"*What*, Marina? What happened?" She tried to sit up—quite impossible; she could hardly get the phone to her ear. Pilar sensed Nancy watched her every move, dark as it was.

"He is OK, not that kind of thing," Marina continued.

"Tell me. I'm taking a mud bath."

"I'm at the store in the mall, in Rancho. I see him with that little faggot Mexican, talking about how they plan to get all the Grecos' money and go away!"

"What?"

"Then Connor buys the little guy perfume bottle! Disgusting!"

Pilar heard rustling behind her head; the mute attendants were back in for the next phase of pamper torture.

"I have to go," Pilar whispered. "We'll talk about it when I get home."

She was about to tuck the phone back into the sheet folds covering her thighs when she noticed a text had come in during the conversation with Marina. It was Jacy: I'M IN THE PARKING LOT, LEFT SIDE. Pilar exhaled, then slid the phone against her flank as the two women once again hovered over her and Nancy.

"You know, Pilar, when you tell me this . . . this crap—about Sy managing things for the tribe, the first honest word that comes to mind is *conspiracy.*"

Pilar shut her eyes and pressed them with all her might deep into her skull, hoping it would make this all disappear.

7

George Gomes wondered if it was normal that twins smelled different.

Because he could swear these two did. Jimbo and Timbo McLaughlin, on the surface so much the same, about as tall as Connor, but so much lighter, *blondie boys*, the both of them, though by now almost the end of summer and they were tan.

All the gringos who worked for the Grecos—including Connor, who was more of a boss, and except that silly Daniel, who was more of a secretary—had muscles; at least, muscles bigger than George's. But these Marines were in a group all by themselves.

In the cab of a Greco truck, George was the passenger and Jimbo drove. Out of the corner of his eye George could see the bulge of Jimbo's arm as he gripped the steering wheel, a bulge that would be hot and tough and smell like chlorine and suntan oil and desert sand if he touched his nose to it.

George wondered what his girl must be like, how she would be the one privileged to do the touching and the smelling and the sighing. They always talked about their girls, these two brothers, sometimes in whispers, often at peak volume with a fair amount of laughter and show. This was a specific male world he'd always felt shut out of, and the fact that these were men of a different country made that division even more overwhelming.

George didn't need to worry about these things at all, because he had his own man, his own Connor, even if it was a secret and even if it was not exclusive. He'd figured out Connor had to do "things" for Sy Greco, sometimes. Because Sy was the boss. That was the only reason. He couldn't, wouldn't love that older man, that horrible older man.

George didn't like it when his thinking went down this way, because inevitably it would lead to imagining the two of them in bed together. This made him feel sick, like he'd puke, the same feeling he got on those little pueblo carnival rides back in Mexico when he was a kid.

Jimbo reached over to turn down the radio, which had turned to talky-talky news anyway, boring, and they always spoke so fast, making it hard for George to get the English. They were headed to one of the Greco projects, this one a house down in the Canyon Country Club area, next to a golf course where they'd turned off the water and all the plants and palm trees were now brittle, brown and dead.

This was a shuttle; Jimbo would explain the task after they got there and hooked up with the other guys already working inside the house, Santiago and Dante. It was nearly five—George hoped this would not be too complicated; it had been a long day and he was tired; he was thinking of the pool; he was thinking of Connor. And he was thinking of Harry Rosen.

Every day, this was always with him, and he was sure something bad was going to happen, but so far nothing had—which made him worry all the more. Why hadn't he insisted that Jacy take the old man to the emergency room? It would have been easy to roll him out of the back of the truck in the hospital driveway and drive off. It was pitch dark by then; nobody would have seen. He'd let the Indian call all the shots and now he regretted it. George had nothing against Mr. Rosen; he seemed like nice old guy (even if he did call him that name he didn't quite understand).

Jacy hadn't been around in close to a week now, and he hadn't seen Nancy Argento either—who had that creepy habit of showing up when he wanted it the least.

They turned the corner and the radio guy was complaining about the president, which was all this particular announcer ever did. It made him wonder why Jimbo always played the same station. It was a broken record.

So they turned onto East Palm Canyon and George saw Harry Rosen, walking away from them, the familiar stooped posture, that crazy pink bald head. His heart pounded; no longer sick to his stomach but panicked. He clutched at the little gray plastic grill covering the AC duct, turning his head to look as they passed.

"Dude!" Jimbo said, hitting George's arm away. "Don't get fingerprints on the clean dash; Sy freaks."

George's heart was going to jump out his mouth, shoot out the window and bounce down the steaming asphalt! But the man was not Harry Rosen. This one was older, if that was even possible.

George remembered Jacy's little dance on top of Mr. Rosen's grave. The dead man was still out there, he was sure, baking in the sand. As much as he'd wanted it to be different, George knew in his soul that Jacy had been right; no hospital would have helped them and if they'd stopped they would have been caught. They did what they had to do.

Jimbo turned down a side street off LaVerne Way. A lot of the houses here were empty because of the "real estate problem" Sy Greco talked about. It wasn't hard to figure out which ones—all the plants in front were dead, and the grass, if there had been any, was now the same color as the sand.

At one of the driveways they stopped. Jimbo cut the engine. George opened the door and the quiet rushed in. The desert always had that effect, but he expected to hear other Greco workers, a hammer pounding, a saw buzzing.

"They should be out in back. I'll be right there," Jimbo said.

George went in the front door, which was closed but not locked. Like so many of the Palm Springs houses the Grecos were working on, this one had mostly empty rooms with supplies stacked precisely on tarps in the corners: paint, lumber, sometimes other items that were a mystery, shrink-wrapped on rough pallets.

Often—and this was the case here, too—there were things left behind by those who had to leave reluctantly and quickly. This house had a green easy chair in what had been the dining room. The upholstery was ripped up the back, but if it were pushed up against a wall no one would know. George wanted to sit there but he heard Jimbo slam the truck's door.

Nobody was in the house. No workers and no noise, no nothing. When he got all the way to the back, the usual sliders led to a pool in the yard. He heard a click as the air-conditioning system kicked in, then felt the light breeze as cool air from a duct floated down.

Jimbo was behind him. George turned to see the Marine standing there with his toolbox.

"Where is everybody?"

Jimbo smiled. He dropped the toolbox on the floor and slid it to the side with his foot, the scratch of sawdust over dirty tile. "Guess they finished up early. Or maybe Daniel got his schedules mixed up."

OK, false alarm, then. He'd get to go home early, wait for Connor in that empty mansion's pool. *This was the life!*

George started back up toward the front door, but Jimbo held out his arm, blocking the way.

"What's the hurry? We could stay for a while. Use the pool. Take it easy."

George's face was hot; his heart pounded in his chest. "Mr. Greco probably has something else he wants me to do."

Jimbo's outstretched arm relaxed, ending up on George's tight flank, where it stayed. "I'm not such a bad guy," he said, so softly it was a whisper. "Everybody thinks I'm a dick, because we were in the military, because we were in Iraq, but I'm not. Maybe my brother is, but *I'm not.*"

George didn't need this. After all the shit, Mr. Rosen, Nancy Argento from the paper, waiting for whatever *pesadilla* was coming next by way of Jacy. But here he was, in an empty house with a Marine who had backed him into a wall.

"What was that like? In Iraq?"

Jimbo's soft smile went away. "I don't talk about that."

"OK, we don't talk about that, then, Jim. Did you leave the phone in the truck? We should get it."

Jimbo's other hand was also now on George, who was being pulled closer. "I'm not such a bad guy," he said again. "The drugs—I sell those to make a living; it's not like I'm really into it at all." He kissed George on the cheek, then on the lips.

George pushed against the bigger man's chest with both hands, but it was a halfhearted effort. Truthfully, there was not much effort at all.

"I really like you, George, but you can't ever tell my brother—or *anyone*."

Jimbo tasted a little like cherry sugar. He'd been drinking out of a plastic bottle with a pink liquid inside—that must be it, another American miracle.

George closed his eyes. He was being lifted; he had no choice but to put his arms around Jimbo, who carried him all the way back to that green chair in the dining room. Then George was on his lap.

He could feel Jimbo's cock hardening under him. His own erection was complete; he couldn't have stopped it even if he wanted to. He opened his eyes and saw a frightened young man.

"You can't tell my brother!" Jimbo said again. "I think I loved you the first time I saw you."

George couldn't listen anymore. He saw Connor. Everywhere. If this had to happen, maybe it was best to think of Connor and imagine it was him.

Jimbo was as careful and gentle as he could be while fucking a guy on the floor of a dirty house under construction. George inhaled dust or sand and convulsed into a sneezing fit. Jimbo held on tighter, giving him a hard forearm for a pillow.

He didn't use a condom and George didn't think to ask about it until Jimbo's cock was already inside. It would be OK; it had been so far with Connor. There was no reason to think this guy wasn't every bit as healthy.

All Jimbo said during the sex was, "Are you OK?" He said this over and over, stroking George's thick black hair, almost like he was his little pet.

George whispered, "Yes."

Yes, I am. Over and over.

Like that it was done, like the sun sinking over that mountain, putting them in the blessed shade. Jimbo held him in his arms and pressed his lips to George's forehead.

That was all the work there was to be had at this Greco house today. Now George wondered, *If these Marines are always talking about the girls they fucked, will Jimbo brag about* this? *Possibly, even, to Connor himself?*

■ ■ ■

Get up here now, he said. *There's a problem, Connor Hurst.*

Connor was in his casita in back of the Grecos' pool. Relaxing, the end of a long day, but they were all long days. He was wearing those slingback cork wedges with an open terry robe, pacing back and forth across the tile. His new pair of snow-white Calvin hip briefs accentuated a tan that got deeper and richer with each passing summer day.

And now here was Timbo, the evil twin. Timbo, insisting he come back up to Morongo, because there was a fucking *problem.*

Duane's awful car, that old Taurus, a new dent every week, was in the Hurst driveway. Connor passed a dusty Jeep a few doors down on Anaconda Lane he recognized as something the twins drove. His mother's truck was nowhere.

It was always quiet out there, but this afternoon was worse. He didn't know; he had this feeling something was wrong. From the outside, everything looked normal, even the way Vi's lavender swayed a bit in the high-desert breeze.

Why wasn't his mother home? If she had to leave for some reason, it was almost always after dinner; she'd been that night person.

The door was open a crack, Timbo behind it. He nodded, leaving the door open but retreating back inside.

Now, Connor didn't want to walk into his family home, but he had to. He didn't have to go far. Duane's body lay in a puddle of red in the hallway leading to the kitchen.

The only thing that cut the quiet was the predictable hum of his mother's ancient refrigerator. There wasn't any point in leaning over to check on his half brother: Duane Gamble was dead; that was clear.

"What the fuck happened?"

Timbo hemmed and hawed and wiped his mouth and shifted his rough hands from front pockets to back pockets, and what he came up with was, "It got away from me, Connor; this wasn't supposed to happen this way."

"No shit. Where's your gun?"

He said he put it back in the Jeep already; yeah—the one down the block.

"You were supposed to take him out past Landers, off road to that wash, don't you remember?"

"Yeah. Of course I do! Except he figured it out, Connor; he knew something was up and he started to accelerate, I mean, run. He was going to exit that back door and get away and call your mother. I had to do *it*."

Connor felt dizzy *and* he had no idea where his mother was right this second: not the best situation by a long shot. Duane had figured out that it was he and Locker skimming Vi; what he had coming was his own fault and inevitable. He'd even looked up the word *fratricide* and realized it didn't technically apply because Duane Gamble was not a Hurst. He knew in his heart it was only a matter of time till Duane came after him.

Then again, this hadn't turned out as planned. He'd do one thing right by his *half* brother and get this psycho Marine out of Vi's house.

"Let's get to work," he said to Timbo.

■ ■ ■

To George Gomes it felt strange to have sex with two different guys in one day, but that was what happened.

They were in bed in "his" bedroom, that wonderful place where the glass walls looked out over Palm Springs, still best at night when the lights sparkled in the town below and up at the tram station on top of Mount San Jacinto.

Connor was quiet after coming and George was exhausted from the day. The city lights were hypnotic, though; he never tired of them. He'd begun to think of this empty house as his own, wrongheaded as that was. He loved coming home to it.

As he rested his hand on Connor's big, protective arm he felt better about what had happened earlier at that other empty house. He had to admit he liked the attention from Jimbo and he liked their sex, too.

Thinking about it again made him quickly hard. Connor's hand arrived to rest on his cock.

"What do we have here?" he whispered in George's ear.

"I thought you were sleeping."

"I can't sleep. I'm worried, *chico*."

George nestled himself closer in, the little spoon. He loved feeling a part of whatever this was, this *conspiración*.

"Sy Greco's a bad man." Connor sighed. "You know that already, what he tried with you, when he thought I didn't know."

"He's a pig," George offered, gratified when Connor pulled him even closer. *This is what he wants to hear.*

But he'd noticed before that Connor was a little different tonight—for him, oddly quiet, subdued. It could've been the weather—the wind had shifted and was bringing in the monsoon from Arizona—the air turned heavy and thick, yet still so horribly hot.

"But he's a rich pig," Connor let out with a cough. Or was it a chuckle? "Haven't told you this, but—when Sy dies, I'll own half of Greco & Greco, Georgie! Half the fucking company, and *you* get to stay in America."

George stiffened, and not in a sexy way this time. "I stay here anyway, that is my plan. That is always my plan, Connor. You know this, right?"

Connor gripped the smaller man's hip. "He'll send you right back to Mexico when he's through with you. That's what he does."

George wriggled out of Connor's embrace to turn around and face him. "You don't know what it's like there. I can't go back. I *won't go back.*"

Connor leaned in to kiss him. "You know what we have to do, don't you?"

■ ■ ■

George couldn't sleep. The water came out of the tap hot but slowly cooled off. He splashed it over his face and chest, diluting the sweat that wouldn't stop coming.

He couldn't believe what Connor had said to him then, about what they'd "have to do." Did he forget about that awful night with Harry Rosen and that fucking crazy Indian Jacy? Did he think George Gomes was a murderer, and it would be easier now to kill another man since he "participated" once before?

Connor was sound asleep, so peaceful, so beautiful. He wasn't troubled. George, however, wasn't ready to go back to bed, knowing he'd just lie there and stare into space, at the ceiling crisscrossed by those yet-un-painted plaster patches. So he went out, naked, beyond the pool, to lean on the railing where he could watch Palm Springs stretched out below.

He wasn't a murderer. But he wouldn't go back to Mexico, to San Sebastián. It was not part of the plan; it was never part of the plan. Connor said they'd be rich together, they'd move in together, maybe even this house right here, this pool, why not? He'd have the money to buy it.

George thought about that little room in the trailer down in Mecca, where he slept on that thin mattress next to his little brothers' bunk beds. The hollow wall that vibrated and cracked each time his mother, Alma Gomez, banged on it with her fist. And he thought about when Sy Greco thrust his cold hand inside George's khakis, like he was entitled to take what he found there.

Across the deck, the pool filter kicked in with its low hum. Ever-widening circles rippled across the surface of the water. George watched them break against the lip of the pool.

■ ■ ■

It was a rare day—the next day, Sunday—when there was no Greco work to be done at all. Connor didn't like to spend much time trolling malls, but today was about making George Gomes happy.

And was he a bad guy? Connor had avoided looking at himself in the mirror, not wanting to notice the things about him that were like

Duane—the big blue eyes for one, that beautiful free gift from the mother they shared. But yes, he was bad; he couldn't deny the bargain he'd made included violence.

Still, he couldn't help but feel pleased, even a little smug. George had fallen right into this plan, which began that day out in Morongo when the Mexican had shown off his terrific aim, a huge surprise.

He was so much like Connor—and he loved money and hated Sy—so he couldn't imagine how anything would go wrong, it was so perfect, the ideal solution to his and Pilar's dilemma.

They were looking into the display windows at Macy's when George asked, quietly, "You have the gun?"

Connor didn't turn, focused as he was on a newly arrived pair of classic black platform pumps on display, but whispered, "No. Timbo."

George grabbed his arm, which Connor shook off. "A gun of the Marines?"

"*Sí.*"

Connor grinned at George, hoping he could get the shorter man to stop looking so worried, to not draw attention to themselves in what was arguably the busiest location in all the desert cities.

But George was already at the next window bank, an electronics store crowded—well, again, as crowded as it gets in Palm Springs—with teenage boys huddled around the incredibly cool new and shiny expensive gadgets on offer.

"Sy has a drink every night before bed; this time it'll have the rufie," Connor said to him, which stopped him from entering the store.

"What?"

"A rufie. It's a drug; it'll knock him out, don't worry. Foolproof."

Maybe George didn't believe him, but he nodded. He began to go along. "By twelve thirty he'll be sleeping," he said.

"They leave the slider screen unlocked," Connor said. "You only need to get by Candy—the Rottie—which isn't a problem because they keep her locked in the kitchen at night." They were in front of a bookstore now. "Look, it's the new Cormac McCarthy."

Neither the name nor the book (*The Road*) registered with George. "I don't like dogs," he said.

He followed Connor into the store, where he picked up one of the new McCarthy books and turned it over. Reading the copy on the back cover—still not looking at George—Connor said, "Then I'll drug the stupid dog, too."

There was a crowd of people in this store, too many to freely converse. George stood there, silent, but Connor could sense wheels were turning. "Look, if you're not up to it—"

"No. You tell me he's a bad man; I can see that. I know he's a bad man." George glanced over the titles on the display table nearby. "This is too hard English. Let's go."

Almost there, Connor thought. George was almost one hundred percent all in; things were moving; things were really happening now. Maybe Connor wasn't the best brother in the world. Obviously not: half brother shot dead yesterday, yet here he was, casually looking at books today.

This was how the world worked. You put plans in motion and you moved on. Except that now George wanted to stop in the perfume shop. Fewer people, mostly the older ladies. Connor stopped first at the Italian counter, sniffed around and dabbed something called Anconia onto his forearm.

George leaned in to sniff it. "I love this; will you buy for me?"

"If you're good."

George lit up with the smile that always slayed Connor. "When do I get it?"

Connor snapped the top back on the cologne bottle and held it behind him, far away from George's reach. "Depends on how good you are."

George whispered, "Yes. I mean the gun."

Connor squinted at the fine print on the package. "We'll go to Italy. We could go there, or Australia. Always wanted to go there, Bondi Beach. The bitch won't know what hit her!"

George cocked his head, opened his eyes wide. "OK," he said, moving to another counter.

So he'd been a little exuberant, felt a few pairs of eyes. Who could blame him, really? He could see this endgame and it was covered in green for him, for him and George together—and was this exciting!

"Buy this for me, Connor. It smells like San Sebastián, salvia, that sage," George said, spraying the fragrance one quick time below his Adam's apple.

So he did. A little weird that Pilar's maid, that horrible Marina Boyko, appeared right in front of him in the checkout line. She didn't say anything, which was normal; but she shot him a little smile, unusual for her. She took her bag; then she left.

Buying the cologne was the least he could do for the favor George was about to perform. He was right about it being pleasing, too: The scent filled the truck's cab as they left the parking lot and headed back up to the house on Southridge.

George put his arm around Connor's neck and licked the skin next to his ear, lightly kissing. "Phone not ringing ever," he whispered. "I think that Nancy reporter lady forgot all about me."

As they pulled into the driveway up on the hill, George asked, "Where will you be when I do this thing?"

"Someplace where lots of people can see me and remember it," Connor said. "Hunter's Bar—you can meet me there when it's over."

■ ■ ■

Locker Hurst got dressed for the occasion, though no one important might see him, just the new real estate agent, but that wasn't the point. That wasn't ever the point.

It was a watershed day, he was sure, bringing a smile to his evenly tanned and freshly moisturized face. His outfit: off-white shirt, short sleeves (it was still August), offset with a light blue polka dot pattern, which from far away was invisible, fitted gray slacks, the lightest cotton he could find, and new espadrilles, leather dyed navy. He felt great and he looked great, sitting there in his car, the one he owned, the ten-year-old

Mercedes sedan that was spotless except for the standard light cover of brown dust unavoidable in the high desert.

His was the only car in the lot in front of this building on Twentynine Palms Highway in Joshua Tree, a high, single-story wood-framed structure with cracking stucco and peeling gray paint. On the right side, there was a small windowed protrusion that served as the retail store for the little ice cream factory that had operated in this building years before.

It was possible Greg Hurst had taken them—he and Connor and their mother, Vi—to this place as youngsters; as it was, ice cream was in short supply in Joshua Tree and ice cream factories unheard of except for this one. But he couldn't be sure. It was difficult to remember what his dad looked like unless Locker stared at an old photo—and they were rare as well, since Greg Hurst was now the first, earlier ex-husband of a woman who had two.

So where was she, this agent, this Marilyn Jeong? Locker had not met her; she was excited and chatty when he expressed interest in the building over the phone. If she didn't show up soon he'd have to get out of the car anyway; it was fast becoming unbearably hot.

To celebrate, he'd started out the day "borrowing" a tiny bit of Duane Gamble's stash, smoking at Vi's round patio table out in back. Duane hadn't been home the night before, which was odd but not unprecedented. Locker then went to his own room, took the backpack stuffed with fifty grand in nicely wrapped packs of twenties and tossed it in the Mercedes's trunk.

He was feeling good but should've taken an extra joint along, as now there was this downtime. Almost as soon as that thought flew through his head, a quiet Prius crushed the gravel only six feet away, sending another rusty wave cloud over his car.

A short Asian woman in heels emerged, keeping her balance with one hand anchored to the car's roof. She laughed. "I hope you're Locker! I had a heck of a time finding this deal."

Marilyn Jeong pulled a big ring of keys from her shoulder bag as they walked to the factory door. Because of her footwear, she kept sinking into the soft, sandy earth, making the short journey tedious. "Oh, not the best choice in shoes this morning." She laughed, hooking her arm into Locker's. "I'm new to the neighborhood; hope you can indulge me."

"Where from?"

"Pasadena; we just moved," she said, finding the right key with absurd speed and giving the old door a shove with her shoulder. "It's a bit more casual out here."

Marilyn stepped aside so Locker could enter. His eyes adjusted, and it was exactly as he'd hoped; if anything, even better. Much better than the photos. "Look at this place," he said, his voice bouncing off the walls like he was onstage in an empty theater.

"It was manufacturing, but the mods you need for a garage are pretty minor, according to this," Marilyn said, shaking the papers she held. "It's surprisingly clean, isn't it?"

They stood in the center. Locker looked up to where skylights sent shafts of light their way. "This is perfect—"

She put a pair of black-rimmed glasses on, her nose close to the sell sheet. "Bathrooms updated to current disability code, saves you money right there."

"I said it was *perfect*."

Marilyn gingerly stepped over to a window facing the back, making a huge racket with those hard shoes. "Good retaining wall out here. There's even a Dumpster they left for you."

"I think I'll take it—"

She turned to him, smiling. "Did you want to set up a viewing with—who is it? Your older brother, the other Mr. Hurst? I could do that later today."

"That won't be necessary. I tried to talk him into it, but—looks like it's just going to be me owning Locker's Garage."

Marilyn literally jumped an inch or so, sending a small cloud of dust up into the empty factory air. "I've got the paperwork out in the car."

"I've got the down payment out there, too," Locker said. "In cash."

Marilyn's eyes widened, her mouth open. She bent over in a fit of giggles. *This woman is so easy to lie to,* Locker thought.

■ ■ ■

But for George Gomes, the on-again, off-again worry about Nancy Argento, her supposed activities and her probable interactions with Homeland Security were never far from his mind and, thus, most often crept in at inconvenient times.

This was one of those. Middle of the night again at the Southridge house, Connor sleeping like a baby *again.*

But not George. Wide-awake, no sleep to be had. Out by the pool yet again, this time with phone in hand, wanting to press the little button that would ring Nancy's phone.

He wanted to shake Connor and scream that Nancy was the real threat. There was something about her that scared him. Guys like Jacy and even Sy were types he was used to, men he might be able to manipulate—Nancy was a mystery.

He sat on the deck and put his legs in the pool, nice and cool in the desert summer night where the temperature was still 90. His phone told the time, just after two A.M.

Maybe she was still at the office. George didn't know, but why not, why would she not be working all night, putting her *diablo* plans to work? Maybe his finger slipped, but he pushed the button and it dialed her number.

The phone rang on the other end. George held his breath, had no idea what he would say. Then came the message: "This is Nancy Argento, *Desert Sun.* Please leave your message."

George took a deep breath in, but before he could even think of the first word to say, the second message, from a man, came through: "This user's voice mail is full. Please try again later."

8

Bitch didn't see the car. Never knew what hit her!

Jacy Martin was sure of it. He saw Nancy Argento's face for that split second before it slammed into her, and it was—no recognition, no surprise, no anything, really. There wasn't time for her to react.

So that's how it ends for the reporter, Jacy thought. *And how will it end for you, Indian? This sure as shit isn't what Pilar Greco asked you to do, though it would be a stretch for anybody to say this here was Jacy Martin's fault. But someone needs to take the blame; someone always has to take the blame for a thing like this.*

She lay there, a heap in the road. A little blond heap with a thin line of bright red blood reaching down to the gutter a few feet away. Fucking murder car didn't even stop. He thought he saw a head of white hair, short white hair, an elderly man most likely, who didn't even register that he'd mowed down a living human being. In a dark BMW, black or navy blue, which now had collision damage to the front: gramps would blame it on a Mexican valet.

Some of these roads in Palm Springs—like the one they were on—were so remote and rarely used that something like this could happen and a person like Nancy Argento could lie there dead or dying for hours before another person passed the same spot.

Thing was, he couldn't just leave her there. He could, quite literally, of course; that would've been his first choice, but Mrs. Greco said, "No, you can't leave her there. Don't be stupid! I have an idea. Put her on the floor in back and meet me at Deepwell."

Even Jacy realized his once green, now dented old Toyota would stick out in the parking lot of a posh joint like Vitaspring. He was only supposed to follow her, report back on where she went or who she met after her spa date with Mrs. Greco.

Like so many things in Jacy's life, this thing backfired, too. Why couldn't he make a little extra money on the side like this? Why were the gods always fucking with him?

Because, of course, Nancy, in her new little silver Focus—even though it was a cheap car, it was new and it was clean and shiny—she wasn't as stupid as Pilar Greco thought and realized Jacy in his shitty car was following her. So she pulled around a corner—first mistake—and went another block or two into a brushy isolated area—second mistake—and then pulled over and got out of her car and confronted the poor little Indian brave—her third and final mistake.

In retrospect, he didn't need to have been so nasty, telling her he had a gun and he was going to use it (which he didn't and he wasn't) and then fake reaching for it under the passenger seat, which was the point where Nancy turned and ran and got run over.

Just like that.

Jacy was surprised at how light she was, easy to lift, even for a small guy like him. He picked her up like she was a baby. She smelled nice, too, just coming from the spa, all those lady-treatment fragrances Pilar Greco had paid for rising around them in the desert air. He giggled, thinking how weird it was that a dead woman would make his horrible crap car smell better.

In his rear view Nancy's own car receded, getting smaller and smaller as he drove away. He'd come back later and push it into the reservation brush.

■ ■ ■

Pilar Greco was happy Connor Hurst did not like expensive whiskey.

She was happy she hadn't wasted much of it on this traitor, and she was thrilled there was more than enough left in the bottle for her hour of need.

She sipped thimblefuls, one after the other, but still, her hands shook—odd, come to think of it, after that nice spa day and the indulgent treatments, which usually so relaxed her.

She lit a votive candle placed in front of the photo of Angel Greco, then lit another. Hoping for his intercession, perhaps; with any luck at all she'd get through this night.

Multiple calls to Connor were made, but she killed them before they had a chance to connect. Their plan for this day had been sealed; they'd agreed not to communicate until after Sy was dead. And she needed to get herself to Laguna.

Over and over in her head, she repeated what Marina had told her: *They plan to get all the Grecos' money and go away.* He would never get his hands on *her* money, unless Sy had done something utterly foolish she didn't know about.

Now Nancy Argento was dead. So unfortunate, the poor girl recently moved from Cleveland, the boyfriend whose golf career had some real wind behind it; now all that was gone.

Angel had indeed interceded. That boy still had his sense of humor, dispatching her via automobile, the very same way he met his own end.

Another thimble of whiskey. A look at the clock, almost three P.M. She had to get out of there; she had to be at the office in Laguna as part of their plan but first had to think of what new things she'd have Marina and Jacy take care of while she was gone. *It could work, this altered plan. You know what? This is genius.*

But first, Sy's safety—he needed to survive this night and she'd only trust that to Marina. But Jacy, and Nancy—

The phone, left on the bed, rang. Her heart thumped when she saw the call was coming from the *Desert Sun.*

Pilar's instinct was to let it go, to ignore it, but she just couldn't. She had to know.

A reporter calling. A guy, Ted something—she didn't quite catch it.

"I'm so sorry to bother you, Ms. Greco," he said. "Trying to track down my colleague Nancy Argento."

A muffled conversation came from the front part of the house. Sy was home, likely talking to Marina.

"How can *I* help you?" Pilar asked Ted.

"That's the thing. Her last Outlook entry has her meeting you this morning at ten, at Vitaspring."

"I treated her to some girl time at the spa. Lovely woman."

Blood rushing past her ears filled the pause that came after.

"She fell off the radar after that, then. She didn't come into the office after lunch; she's not answering her cell or any texts."

Pilar sat down on the bed. "Let's see. We left the spa about twelve thirty. Hard to remember the exact time; we were so . . . relaxed. She followed me out of the parking lot in that little car of hers."

"That's what the valet out there said."

"I'm sure she's out tracking down a lead. She was working on a bunch of stories. Did you check with her boyfriend, that golfer, what's his name, Eddie?"

"No. He's in Europe, on a tour. Ernst. He won't be back for weeks."

Pilar went to the slider and rolled it shut. She let out a little laugh. "She called me from her car to thank me again for Vitaspring. Nancy will likely dance through the door any moment."

■ ■ ■

Sy decided on a new blanket edict for Greco & Greco: no remodels down valley east of Palm Desert. It was too difficult to get to—the area was growing, good for everybody, sure, especially for realtors—but with all the new people came new traffic, and he never had much patience with that.

It was already late enough, and he'd asked Marina if she wouldn't mind stopping by a property in La Quinta where he had to check some electrical before he could drop her back in Palm Desert. He had to get there before dark; no utilities were hooked up yet.

She'd pleaded; her own car, the boxy old Volvo, wouldn't start; it was stuck there in Deepwell on Ocotillo in front of their house. She'd even take the fucking Sun Bus over in the morning; she had a Russian friend who knew a mechanic. It wouldn't be a major fix.

But the car was dead today, dead tonight. Pilar would be on her way to Laguna for the night, so she couldn't do it. In fact, she insisted. Though Sy knew if he got back in a decent amount of time, he'd be able to spend the evening with Connor.

So Marina Boyko brought her things with her, piled her two big bags in the back (why did she come to work every day loaded for a two-week cruise?), except for the minicooler she used as an oversized lunch box.

"How far is drive to this house?" she asked, looking away from him toward the barren, sizzling hills to the south.

Marina was not ugly by any means, though her simple modified page-boy cut was a little pedestrian for the desert. Still, Sy thought it—and the blond dye job—attractive. She might even have a man in the complex whom she spent time with but never mentioned.

"There's not much traffic. Twenty minutes, maybe less."

"Good. I must worry about my sugars," she said, opening up the cooler and taking out a chilled liquid in a plastic bottle, which she shook. "I make smoothie at home and look forward to it all day."

It smelled of apple and citrus. She took a sip and brushed her lip with her fingers.

"You don't happen to have anything else in there, do you? Water or something?"

Marina looked in the cooler. "There's a water." She took it out; he reached for it; she pulled it back. "Mr. Sy, you're driving. I open it for you."

■ ■ ■

Back in San Sebastián, George Gomes had grown up with a belief that identical twins had a power, a certain magic. A person would mess with that at his own peril. Along with that uneasy *peligro* in the presence of twins was the conviction that no one, not even their mother, could always tell them apart.

But perhaps this natural law did not apply in America, for he found it easy to distinguish between Timbo and Jimbo McLaughlin.

Jimbo was the big, almost shy protector who wanted his approval; that showed in a man's eyes. But Timbo!

There was something wrong with Timbo. He'd noticed it before when he'd catch the man looking at him, or at somebody else, often with that odd, crooked smile he had.

Like he was plotting or planning or just about to say or do something. That wouldn't be pleasant.

Timbo was like that earlier when George picked up the gun, laughing, making a stupid joke: "Do I have to show you how to load this, *chico?*"

The way Connor had talked, George thought it was going to be some special armed forces of the United States weapon—a gun of the Marines— but it wasn't. It was just a Glock, the regular kind he'd shot in Mexico, the same gun he used when they practiced in Vi's backyard.

Timbo's snickering faded from his mind as George turned into the Deepwell neighborhood. He drove one of the Greco company trucks. Connor had said, "Nobody's gonna notice a Greco truck in front of their house—it's perfect." Still, it made George nervous as he had only his fake license on him and to be picked up meant a one-way ride to Mexicali.

Like all Palm Springs nights, this one was dead quiet except for a few crickets. The truck's clock said 12:33. He turned off the motor and the lights and the world was asleep.

George pulled on the plastic gloves Connor had left on the passenger seat. He didn't close the driver's door; he wouldn't make any more noise than was absolutely necessary.

The Grecos' front garden lights were on. The house itself was dark. Hooking the gun into his waistband, George hoisted himself over the three-foot slump-stone wall. He could make out the pathway that led around the house to the unlocked slider in Sy's bedroom.

He'd been at the Grecos' before, always during the day, when there was activity, loud talking, other crew and always this nervous busyness. It was so peaceful here in the dark, simply somebody's house, somebody's sleeping house. So much nicer than that Mecca trailer, not even in the same category, not even in the same fucking universe.

And also not in the same universe as his own new house, that one in the hills overlooking Palm Springs with the infinity pool where he contemplated his future. Which was a bizarre way to think, but there was no doubt he was living in it even if he had no official "paperwork."

This was going to be so easy. There was no one around; Sy was a bad, bad man who had bad plans for George; Connor would inherit all this and they'd go away and be happy. He pushed the faces of his little brothers Jesse and Chuy out of his head. After tonight they'd have to find other role models. He could no longer accept that duty.

If there was a sense of loss to that, maybe he'd feel it tomorrow. Right now his heart pounded like it was going to jump out of his throat. As he made the turn at the corner of the house, he heard a deep growl and could see the outline of a dark mass directly in front of him on the pathway.

Candy. Connor had *promised* he'd take care of the dog!

But there she was, sitting motionless, blocking his path.

"Doggie, honey, quiet, OK?" George whispered.

Candy moved toward him a foot or so and stopped. George dared not take another step. He pulled the gun out of his pants.

His words to calm the dog had the opposite effect. She crouched lower, her growl sustained. Somebody was gonna hear this; somebody would come.

He gave it another try, this time in Spanish: *"Tranquilo, tranquilo . . ."*

Which appeared to work. The dog lay on the pathway tiles, keeping her eyes on George.

He took a small step forward.

And she lurched.

Not at the speed of light; it was the speed of darkness from its very heart. It happened so fast the pop the gun made didn't even register. Candy collapsed with a pathetic squeak an inch from his toes.

It took George a moment to catch his breath. The silence of the night remained. No lights had come on; no one was coming. Even the crickets had stopped chirping.

He nudged Candy with his toe. No response. Convinced she wouldn't move—ever again—he stepped over her lifeless form. The Greco house and Sy's unlocked slider door were only ten feet away.

The unexpected clash with the dog left George trembling. He'd always liked animals. They couldn't have a dog at the rented dump of a trailer in Mecca, but years earlier, when he was a kid in Jalisco, they'd had a couple of Chihuahua mixes. Strays would simply find their door.

How could you kill a dog, asshole? His heart pounded in his ears, not even thinking in that particular moment he was about to kill a *man*.

Other than a night-light casting an amber glow from the master bath, there was no light in the bedroom. Hand shaking, George pushed the slider door to the right. It slid soundlessly on the straight, clean, perfectly lubed track.

The edge of a sheer drape on the inside billowed out and hit George in the face. The air-conditioning was on, of course. The internal breeze it created escaped.

George brushed the fabric aside and turned his head one last time to make sure Candy hadn't come back to life. Her dark outline remained on the pathway leading to the front of the house. He could step inside.

He'd opened the slider just enough so he could slip in sideways. He held his breath until his eyes adjusted—which took only seconds.

The room was big, bigger than he'd imagined. There was a seating area, a sofa and chairs, right inside the slider doors. Along another wall were the doorways to the his-and-hers bathrooms / dressing rooms Connor joked about. At the far end were the raised platform and the Greco bed.

Other than the almost undetectable hum of the forced air, there was no sound. George guessed Sy was one of those men, that rare minority, who did not snore.

He wondered if Sy slept naked. Why this made any difference for what he was about to do he wasn't sure, but he was certain there wasn't time to delay. The longer he stood, the more likely Sy was going to wake up or some other distraction would wreck this.

George took another step forward. He was at the base of the platform and could make out the mounds and ridges Sy's body made under a thin cover sheet. As he raised the gun and steadied his right wrist with his left hand, there was a sharp clattering off to his right.

He jumped.

He shot—or the gun went off—into the wall above the bed, shattering the plaster.

He re-aimed, shot into the bed. Then he unloaded one last bullet for insurance.

Sy hadn't moved before and certainly wasn't moving now. Even in the dark, George saw a black pool of blood radiating onto the sheets.

He stepped up onto the platform.

"Stop. Stop right there." Sconces along the wall powered on.

It was Connor. Had he been hiding in one of the bathrooms? He had his own gun, pointed right at George!

"What you doing?"

Connor shook. "You broke in. You fucking killed my partner."

George lowered his gun, pointing it to the floor.

"Connor?"

He couldn't believe the man he loved was going to end it like this. He stood there, not moving, not daring to breathe. He saw Jesse and Chuy's disgusted faces, wishing he'd had at least one more chance.

After a few interminable seconds, Connor exhaled. He lowered his gun.

A look passed between them. George had never wanted to fuck him more than right that second. Sick—a bleeding body was only six feet away. He giggled.

Connor nodded toward the bed. "Let's make sure he's dead."

With the lights now on, George could see that Sy had a sheet over everything, head included.

"Wait." Connor laid his gun on the dresser. George went to him, leaving his own weapon beside the other, and embraced him. They kissed, but Connor broke free.

"You need to make sure his eyes are closed. I can't do this," Connor whispered.

"Let's get out of here."

Connor grabbed his arm. "Check."

"OK, OK, let go of me." Sy's bedside clock glowed 12:50. George couldn't believe all this had gone down in only twenty minutes.

He used the tip of his forefinger and thumb to pull on the sheet at the head of the bed. It floated back.

George gasped. *What* was nosy reporter Nancy Argento doing in Sy and Pilar Greco's bed?

■ ■ ■

Jesus fucking Christ, Connor thought.

"Nancy?" George gasped.

The two of them stood there on either side of the bed, in the semi-dark, the light from the sconces streaking over Nancy's body, her pretty blond hair now stained with her own bright red blood.

Connor's head spun. Where the fuck was Sy? Pilar had gone ahead and changed the rules here, and he felt his head was going to explode.

The way George looked at him sideways, the understanding of betrayal that was about to go down, was more than he could bear. The ridiculous picture of him pointing a gun at George only reinforced how much he had grown to love this man.

"I'm sick," George said.

"Take it easy—"

"How can I take it easy? Was one thing, Connor, maybe kill a bad man and get his money; it's a really bad thing to shoot a girl—like this one."

"Who is this?" Connor asked, taking out his phone. He'd call that bitch Pilar; he'd get an answer right away.

"Nancy! The newspaper writer I keep telling you about."

Connor couldn't very well admit to George that the original plan had been for the Palm Springs cops to find two bodies in this bedroom, murder victim Sy and murderer George Gomes, *aka* Jorge Gomez, shot in self-defense by one Connor Hurst, the upstanding young tenant on the Greco property.

No, that would not do at all. A dead reporter in this bed was much more problematic. She would have to go away. He tucked his phone into his back pocket. If he tried Pilar's number now he understood it wouldn't go anywhere.

"We have to get rid of her, get rid of the body," Connor said.

"Let's get out of here and leave her."

Connor coughed. "Remember, dude, I live out in the casita. I'm the first guy they'd haul in."

George glanced down at the body, then locked eyes with Connor. "I can try to remember the way out to Harry Rosen," he said.

Connor jerked his head to the side and up—as if he was looking toward the mountain out in the darkness. "I have a better idea," he said. "But we need to be quick."

George backed the Greco & Greco truck up to the garage, while Connor removed the translucent shower curtain from his casita bathroom, ripping it off the rail, rings scattering across the tiles.

While he was back in the casita he texted Pilar. A simple WTF?? It took great restraint not to add the words *bitch, cunt* or both, because if any situation warranted cursing, this was it.

And where was Sy? If he wasn't rufied, passed out in this bed, then where was he? He could show up any second. They had to leave, immediately, with Nancy.

From the garage rafters, the two of them pulled down a blue tarp used when the occasional winter rain made the roof leak. They covered Nancy Argento's shower-curtain-wrapped body with it and laid it in the truck bed. Then they gingerly placed a new slab of drywall over it. *Just in case.* The Palm Springs police could stop them for anything—you never knew; someone had told Connor they were back in town filming that "reality" show *Cops.*

It was about eight miles from the Deepwell house to the Mountain Tramway Station.

Connor wondered how smart George really was—how much he'd be able to put together about how badly their little murder plot was playing out.

If he assumed they were going to bury Nancy somewhere in the desert, the turns toward the mountain and the slow rise in elevation would convince him otherwise.

He didn't know if George had been up there before. Certainly not with him, though passing the giant glowing sign with the arrow "Palm Springs Aerial Tramway" would be impossible to miss.

And he didn't. "Why we going to the mountain?" George asked, his voice the quiet whisper of someone exhausted.

He hadn't been in the room when Connor made the call to Jacy. He'd been sent to the garage to find that tarp. He sure wasn't going to be happy to see the Indian up at the tram.

"Trust me. There's way more places up on that mountain to hide something," Connor said, as if it was the most obvious thing to do, as if carting around a dead body in the back of the truck was an everyday kind of thing.

"There's bears up here," George said, looking out the window into the brush, which thickened as they approached the base station elevation. "Mountain lions."

Connor didn't like driving on curved roads like this in the dark, especially out of the city where it was pitch black. George was right—anything could be out there.

"That's the point, George. She won't lie around for long up there."

Pilar hadn't called back or texted. This was the problem with women, and Connor had it reinforced one more time. No matter if it was your lover or your mother, sooner or later you just couldn't trust them.

Something had gone so wrong! He tried to remember the only part of this game that mattered—where the money was and how soon it would be in his possession.

But why had she pulled this?

He was forced to stop thinking at the next bend, as the tram station came into view. Only essential electricity was on after midnight, giving the place an unsettling dim glow. It was located at the base of a steep canyon on Mount San Jacinto; the station lights accentuated the cottonwoods and shards of the sheer granite walls as well as the tram cables, which angled up, then disappeared into the dark.

The parking lot was empty except for the tribe's restaurant supply truck with the huge Montana Grande logo on its side—this one an enormous Native American man staring right at them, judgmental and accusatory, as if the spirit of the mountain knew exactly what they'd done and what their own cargo was. There was a car parked next to it, nearly colorless in the dark, but the dust and the dents had Jacy Martin written all over them.

A couple of other Indians—Paco and some other guy—unloaded food boxes from the truck, destined for the restaurant at the top of the mountain. Connor didn't have to look at George to know his jaw dropped as soon as he saw Jacy.

"You fucker, what's *he* doing here?"

Connor switched off the ignition. "Calm down. Let's get through this."

Jacy nodded, pulled his phone out of his pocket and turned toward the mountain to answer it, walking into the darkness out of their line of sight.

"He was coming here all along. *Who* was it you were gonna dump up there, Connor? Was it *me*?"

This had all unraveled so quickly and completely, if there was a point to continued lying, Connor wasn't sure what that would be. "Let's get her out of the truck," he said. "At least I didn't *shoot* you, George."

■ ■ ■

It was like everything moved in slow motion, and the sound came from a speaker somewhere in the back of a big, empty room. You could hear it but it didn't make much sense. George couldn't get his head around it, but he figured his unquestioning trust of Connor was gone.

Then there was Jacy. That squirrely little murderer bounced off the steel and glass walls of the brightly lit tramcar, where he directed Paco and his buddy to stack the boxes of frozen French fries and cola syrup.

George didn't want to say anything more to Connor, but he needed to know what to expect. They'd both left their guns stashed under the truck's front seat, then eased Nancy's body out of the back. She landed with an unintended thud on the cracked asphalt next to the loading dock.

"I got the spot for coyotes," Jacy said. "It's not far up at all." He grinned and nodded to George, as if they were in a conspiracy to keep secrets—though what had happened to Harry Rosen was no longer any secret in this group.

Every time he glanced at Jacy—whether the little man was lord-
ing it over Paco, peering at Nancy under the tarp and giggling, or fid-
dling with the tram control panel like he knew what he was doing—all
George saw was his creepy little dance on top of Mr. Rosen's sandy
grave.

How could it be that he, *Jorge Gomez*, had been involved in the killings
of two people when he hadn't planned any of this, when all he ever wanted
was to get some money and a sexy American man in the process?

Jacy, Paco and the other guy finished stacking the boxes in the tram
and stepped back onto the platform. "Room for her right here by the
door," Jacy said, pointing to the empty spot. He glanced up at the big
clock on the station wall. "It's eleven after, a good number to start this.
Let's go."

Blood dripped off the shower curtain and off the blue tarp into the
dirt around the tram. They hoisted Nancy onto the slim loading dock,
then laid her body on the tram deck near the door, the same floor dozens
of fat tourists would stand on in the daylight hours to come.

Jacy's phone went off. "It's Kaya again. Just a minute, guys." He slipped
between Connor and George and hurried into the station proper.

Connor shook his head. Paco and the other Indian—whose name
George finally remembered as Vinnie—left the tram to load empty boxes
back into the truck.

"Everybody's going to know about this," George said, watching the
two boys. "This is so fucked."

Jacy returned from the station after only a couple of minutes, his call
quite brief after all. "Let's get on up that mountain," he said.

Jacy muttered something to Paco and Vinnie in the Indian language
neither George nor Connor could understand. It seemed *involved*. The boys
nodded, got in the truck and pulled away, heading down the hill back to
town.

"What did you say to them?" George asked, his eyes on Nancy's lifeless bulk. He stepped over her, Connor following, giving Jacy a push.

"Told the boys to park the truck in back of the casino. What do you
think I told them? What the fuck is your problem, *Jorge*? Who do you think

you are, questioning me?" Jacy sat in the center console, flicked a switch or two, and the tram hummed to life.

"Shut up," Connor said, moving his hand out of the way just as the tram doors slid closed. "It's bad enough we have to do this. We don't need you two fighting."

The tram lurched forward, then swung back, breaking free from the station landing. George held on to one of the steel support poles so he wouldn't fall into the boxes or onto Nancy.

There was that momentary odd sensation of weightlessness, made stranger by it being so dark outside, what he imagined outer space must be like.

A rocket ship to hell, that's what this was. The tram leveled out, began to rise, and hadn't gone far at all when Jacy cut the power.

"Now what?" George didn't know if he'd ever seen Connor so nervous.

It was silent except for the tiny whine of the tram gear on the cable above as they all swayed back and forth in the dark.

"We're on the edge of a ravine where the doggies come down every night. Good place to dump her," Jacy said.

He pushed a button. The doors closest to George slid open.

Best to get this over with as soon as possible; then the forgetting can begin, George thought. He bent down to drag Nancy to the edge. He'd just pulled up on the tarp, got a good grip, when Jacy knocked him back on his ass. He dropped the body, a thin line of red now snaking out the door into the mountain void.

"That was Mrs. Pilar Greco on the phone, you asshole!" Jacy spat— not at him, but at Connor.

It was light enough so George could see Connor's face burn red. "So *you've* got a hotline to the boss? That what you're saying, Jacy?"

"When you fuck with the Grecos, man, you fuck with me!"

Jacy lurched at Connor. George wanted to run—but where? He could hardly move as it was. Jacy and Connor, locked together, hit the tram wall, making the car swing.

George's gut dropped to his ankles. The sway tumbled a stack of box-es. One came to rest on top of the blue tarp covering Nancy; another fell out the open door.

Connor and Jacy lunged to the opposite side, barely missing George. Connor, the bigger and stronger, fell on top of Jacy. He pushed his head out the tram doorway.

Didn't seem to matter, though. Jacy punched him in the face—first left, then right. "You motherfucker!" Connor screamed, squeezing his fin-gers around Jacy's scrawny little throat.

Then Jacy hooked his hands under Connor's arms, pushing him up, which in this case was out the doorway. George dove in to grab Connor by the belt, which only pulled his pants down and did nothing to keep his body in the tram.

Jacy got the stupidest look on his face, realizing momentum was in his favor and he'd win this.

Connor had now pushed Jacy's shoulders out the door as well as his head. With one loud grunt, Jacy pushed with his arms and thrust up with his legs, pulling both himself and Connor out the door.

The only sound was the tiny, insignificant squeak the tramcar made as it swung on its cable. Nancy's body had rolled during the fight; a pale arm protruded from the blue shroud. Stepping over her, George looked out the tram door into the black night.

They weren't as high off the mountain as they could've been further up the cable. Even in the dark, George made out the tops of trees below, the tamarisks or cottonwoods that grew alongside the creek.

■ ■ ■

Marina Boyko called Pilar to tell her that her instincts were again correct, like always, and it appeared true that Connor had removed Nancy Argento from the Grecos' Deepwell home.

"Totally appeared" was the best she could verify: He and the little Mexican had carried something that resembled a rolled-up rug out of the house. It was pitch black on the street, after midnight, the result of the light-pollution ordinances of the local government, so there were limits on what even she could see.

But seriously, who moved rugs in the dark in the middle of the night? *No one, no one is doing that,* Marina told her. It had to be Nancy.

Pilar's hand shook as she wrote out the check to Marina. She hadn't planned on having to rely so much on this woman, this maid, presumed loyal yet from a country known for its treachery. Though she could not admit it right then, right there, Pilar knew there'd be many more payments like this one made in the future, and she hated that idea.

Whatever it turned out to be, she'd think about it some other time. Right now she had to get back, back to the desert to salvage what she could of the cash she could get before Connor or, heaven forbid, Sy got his filthy hands on it.

Pilar formulated her new Plan B during a quick midnight walk on the beach, steps away from Greco & Greco's Laguna office on Ocean Avenue. This OC outpost over a juice bar consisted of two rooms, the office itself and a back room Sy had converted into a studio apartment with a bed and a sofa and a beige Suzy Homemaker kitchen Pilar thought was ghastly. *I won't have to look at this again, ever.*

She couldn't sleep—that was a nonstarter—so why not walk? Her intuition told her that this reporter Ted was not going to let go. How, in any reasonable reality, could they ever explain what they'd done in what started out as a simple hit-and-run-victim scenario? It was insane. It was not explainable.

So she'd get out of town, let things cool off, come back in a year or so. A sabbatical. Let Sy handle Ted's questions—he was clueless anyway. She'd need to stop at home and pack some things, go to the office for the money, then make her way to the airport.

Since it was summer, people were still hanging around the beach at night, even this close to dawn. She'd touch her feet to the mild surf and begin the drive back. There'd be little traffic at this hour; Pilar could be home in Palm Springs in a couple of hours. Soft moans came from a dark mass moving just to the left on the sand. Did her presence cause them to worry or pause in their lovemaking? She hoped so—it wasn't fair what Connor had done to her, and some cosmic retribution was in order, even if things didn't work that way.

■ ■ ■

Sy came to when the August sun climbed far enough into the sky to blast through the window and set his face on fire. There was the usual morning back pain he'd accepted as a fact of life for a man of sixty, but today this bed was unforgiving.

He swallowed, tongue scratching the dry roof of his mouth. Then Sy realized he was not in a bed and was not in his house.

He pushed himself up; the room spun. He'd slept on a bare floor, clothes on. The room was empty except for the slabs of drywall leaning against the old wood framing. Sy assumed he had fallen onto the floor where he woke but a quick inspection revealed no marks, at least none he could see.

He was in one of the company's remodel projects. In fact, this was the La Quinta house. Now he remembered driving down Highway 111 on his way here—with the maid, with Marina.

What the fuck had happened? And where was she?

The company truck was right there out in the driveway; he could see it through the empty windows. Solution: Call Connor and get a quick answer. But his phone, fished out of his pocket, was dead. There was no charger. He could try to find a pay phone, but then—he didn't have any change.

On his way back home up Palm Canyon Drive—trying to make good time, but with little luck; he'd hit what morning rush the desert cities had—Sy tried to piece it together. Irritated Marina was so disorganized. She could've used her resources at the Grecos' Deepwell house to get her fucking car fixed so she wouldn't have had to bother him for a ride.

He knew she was a health nut, made those juice shakes, always a vile shade of green he could not imagine drinking. She carried a picnic cooler—did she really bring it to work with her every single day?

She did. Lunches and snacks; Marina couldn't trust that Pilar would have anything healthy on hand. That part was true; he could hardly blame the maid for his wife's shortcomings.

So they were having juice and he didn't remember what happened after. His objective had been to connect the utilities at the La Quinta house; that had failed.

Unless. What had she done? Sy's lids were still heavy, yet he felt like he was sitting two inches above the driver's seat. His head throbbed. He hadn't had to look for a pay phone in years and most were now gone; halfway back he figured it would be easier to wait till he got home rather than ask a stranger for coins.

Sy pulled into the driveway at Deepwell. He let himself in through the side gate. It was always so quiet in Palm Springs on summer mornings, part of the attraction. But at his house Candy would always be waiting; she knew Master was returning when he was still blocks away.

Sy turned at the side of the house on the path that led to the pool in back, and he saw her there: from far away, an unmoving mound of dark fur.

"Candy?"

She lay in a sticky pool of blood, still, lifeless. He bent to stroke her. He had to get out of the sun or he would puke.

The sliders to their bedroom were open a foot or so. Inside, everything looked usual; the bed had been stripped. There was no sign of his wife or Marina or anyone else.

"Pilar!" he shouted. No answer came, the only sound the constant hum of the air-conditioning system.

He stumbled back outside, along the pool deck leading to the casita. He pounded for Connor on the guesthouse door. Again, no response. Sy wedged his shoulder against the locked door, but the good money he'd spent on premium hardware did its duty and the damn thing didn't budge.

With each additional moment of silence, Sy felt his guts churn, the unavoidable conclusion mounting that he'd been had—not only had he been drugged by his cunt maid, but the long and amiable détente with his wife was over.

He guessed "being a wife who didn't have to really be a wife" was no longer acceptable and she needed more. Here was the evidence. Time to call the lawyers in Century City. But first he had to find Connor, find out what had happened to Candy.

As he plugged his dead phone into the charger on his home office desk, he saw Marina through the window out at the curb with two gray suitcases—Pilar's suitcases.

Next to Marina's "dead" car, now mysteriously idling. She was trying to maneuver one of the cases into the trunk when he caught her.

"Where's my wife?" he screamed.

■ ■ ■

George would cry later and then light some candles. He'd find some of that cedar incense he knew Connor loved. He'd remember a Spanish prayer and say it.

How long had it been since he got off that bus from Mecca and met Connor Hurst in that parking lot? Not much more than a month. George still couldn't believe he'd gone from living in a shitty old trailer to living in an empty mansion in the hills over Palm Springs, all within a matter of hours.

Now the people he'd met, the characters he'd gotten mixed up with—especially that Jacy, but also Nancy and the beautiful Connor—were gone. It was up to George now, and he'd have to figure out how to continue this big plan.

Which was, of course, to get Greco money. And, in his particular case, to avoid the Homeland Security people. He giggled. Now that Nancy Argento was at the bottom of a San Jacinto canyon full of coyotes, he didn't think *that* was going to be a problem!

He'd done it himself. Killing her was a horrible accident and something he hadn't intended, but George was practical enough to understand he needed to get over that remorse before it made him slip up or, even worse, self-destruct.

He sat in that tramcar—in shock—for several minutes, which seemed like hours—till the damn thing stopped swaying. Then it was just him and Nancy there and that was not going to work out.

He had watched Jacy operate the thing. All he did was push a button; it wasn't like there was any other traffic. George moved the tramcar up the mountain a bit more, stopped it, and rolled her out the door, blue tarp and all.

Buenas noches, Nancy. He'd say a prayer for her, too.

Now he was back down at the station; so simple, it was the other button! This was all so easy. Maybe it was a dream, partly good but partly horrible.

It was still dark. No one else was around; Jacy had made sure of that. Which made the whole thing creepy. George was sure Indian spirits were about; this land was sacred to the tribe. Now there were three fresh souls to join them.

He shivered. A chorus of coyotes yipped and howled on the hillside above him. George grasped the small silver cross he sometimes wore around his neck; he'd put it on today.

The tram station made its own odd settling noises. George imagined the hillside beneath was alive, not only with earthquake faults but with Jacy's ancestors—who couldn't be happy with the evening's events. They were ordering him to leave.

Once you start something, you keep going. Hadn't Alma Gomez said that to him, many times, when he didn't want to go to those horrible camp schools, when he didn't want to practice those stupid English tapes?

She knew how to make the most of a bad situation and had taught her son well.

He had to get away from the tram right now; he didn't know how early the tribal employees showed up for the day's work, but they'd be here before he knew it.

So there was Jacy's car—that dented, colorless piece of shit. Right next to the Greco truck, which he had keys for. Leaving Jacy's would be a huge red flag, but what could he do? There was no ravine to push it into, no gallon of gas to blow it up with (like *that* wouldn't cause attention).

His beautiful man Connor. Dead up there on the mountain, for sure. Or was he? How far did they fall? George didn't know. The trees under the tram blocked the view below. He didn't hear a sound after they fell out the door, other than the coyotes, later on. No screams, no moans, no nothing.

Connor had always been a fantasy man anyway, right? This big, gorgeous, hunky guy with an empty mansion for him to live in, the jobs, the money and, of course, all the sex.

George shed two tears, one from each eye, both for Connor. Jacy would not get grief, not from him. The Indian brought this on himself, killed Connor in the process: no pity and no love.

Predawn gray light had come. He'd roll down the hill back into Palm Springs, rest for a couple of hours in the Southridge house before resuming the search for the rest of the money.

Because if Connor even left a will—which he didn't—surely he'd leave every earthly thing to George Gomes.

■ ■ ■

When George got back to the house, it was silent, like always. The unrelenting quiet of the empty place always surprised him, as if he expected it would someday change. He clocked maybe *tres horas* of sleep, waking up to experience those delightful few seconds of forgetting the awful events of the night before. Then he remembered: three people dead.

If there had been anything at all in his stomach, he would have puked.

The office guy, Daniel, opened up Greco & Greco headquarters at nine. Would Pilar be there? What would he say? After all, she expected him to be dead, for sure, a stupid dead Mexican, according to their idiotic plan. He needed a plan of his own. All he could think of was that cactus, that safe in the shape of a cactus behind Daniel's desk, full of more money that was still in there and rightfully his.

He knew where that key was and he knew the codes, but to get into it he'd have to get Daniel out of there for at least a few minutes.

He also had to return the company truck. With each passing minute, someone somewhere would figure out Jacy Martin and Nancy Argento were gone. To miss Connor might take a little longer.

Daniel was indeed at his desk, as usual, and dressed up, as usual. On a day that was anything *but* usual. He cocked his head to one perfectly positioned side when George entered.

"*Somebody* had a rough night," he said.

"I didn't have no time to take a shower."

Daniel's bow tie was blue with yellow dots. His lips flattened out into a sneer. "The Grecos don't go for that kind of thing, George. You want to make a good impression here. I mean, look at that shirt."

Daniel had turned into the kind of man George would like to hit, but he didn't want to be that kind of angry guy. Then again, he'd just shot a woman. So—maybe he shouldn't bet on what might happen.

"Is Mrs. Pilar here today?"

Daniel exhaled as if he were being so bothered by his presence, when it appeared, at least to George, that nothing *at all* was going on in that office.

"She's at the Laguna property today."

George's focus had moved from Daniel to the atrium behind him, to the little cactus exhibit that held the safe. For an instant he thought, *Why stop now?* though he did have enough sense to remove both guns from the Greco truck and leave them at Southridge.

He'd have to fight Daniel and win, and who knows who else was lurking in the back of the office. Absolutely: there was no guarantee.

But he'd have to figure something out, and do it soon.

George backed away from Daniel, turned and ran out.

"Hey, wait!" Daniel shouted, waving a piece of paper. "Your work list—*here*."

9

The money itself was filthy. Kaya knew—she looked it up on the computer, on Google, to find out exactly what she was getting on her hands every day at the family business. Food poisoning, skin infections, antibiotic-resistant bacteria—the flesh-eating kind, the kind that got your arm amputated, what she had seen on TV while waiting for Andreas to come home. The substance and product of her profession; she could hardly avoid it.

So she'd started wearing tight plastic gloves, which made it simpler to handle the cash, so why didn't she think of this before? The stress, probably. The stress of living with that fat and scary man in the main office, the stress of carrying on this affair with Jacy that was going—yes, nowhere, *admit it to yourself, Kaya*, that's where it was going.

That nagging feeling, that he was with her only for the money and the access, still bothered her, mainly when he wasn't around to distract her. He couldn't keep his shaky little hands on much of it anyway, like they'd planned. It was supposed to accumulate. The nest egg was the only way to ever get forever free of Andreas's claws.

She hadn't seen Jacy yet today and she was certain he was on the schedule. Or maybe she'd gotten it wrong; he was so busy with the Greco remodels, his shifts on the casino floor got fewer and shorter.

Kaya dealt blackjack today, which made her think about how dirty the cards were. Like the paper money. *You'll drive yourself crazy if you focus on that!*

They *had* to be cleaner. They were required to change decks every three hours anyway, more often if someone won too often and counting was suspected. Even so, she kept little bottles of hand sanitizer at her booth in the cash cage as well as in her locker.

A chubby boomer couple had been at her table for about twenty minutes. They were clueless about the desert, visiting in August, but did have some skill at the game.

Did Kaya realize that Dubuque, Iowa, had riverboat casinos? *No, I didn't know that!* she lied. Customers liked being smarter than the dumb Indians. Good for tips; it worked every time.

Then he was there, that Paco, her distant cousin. Standing, not moving, his mouth hanging open, like some stupid statue. Staring at her from half a room away. He was dirty, messy, exactly the opposite of what Andreas told "family" they should look like when in Montana Grande.

She'd always thought he was a bad influence on Jacy, the kind of friend you didn't want someone close to you with a propensity for mischief to hang out with because you knew they'd get into more trouble. But the dweeb just stood there.

"We want some good Mexican while we're here," Mrs. Boomer said.

She expected Kaya to answer. Paco started his walk toward the table as she spread her lips over her teeth in her perfect Indian maiden smile. "You'll love our buffet! It has a super Mexican section."

Mr. Boomer looked up from his cards when Paco arrived, likely expecting him to join in the game.

But he did not sit. Instead, he went around the table to where Kaya stood, a forbidden move in any casino.

In her peripherals she could already see security coming toward them from two directions, and caught the whir of a ceiling cam as it pivoted to focus on her.

"Paco, you can't be here—"

"Jacy lost up on the mountain," he said to her, not in English but in Ivia, the language of their ancestors, now nearly forgotten over this land defiled by the casinos. She flinched, as if shocked, not expecting to hear that message and most assuredly not in that way.

The boomers were more curious than annoyed that their game had stopped. Of course, they couldn't understand what he'd said, but they caught his next sentence: "He hit his head on some rocks and he's dead."

Security was upon them. "You—outta here," the guard said, grabbing his arm, but Paco shook him off.

Kaya's mind raced, disjointed but not enough to forget that she couldn't leave without locking her drop box. She turned the double key and pushed Paco away.

"Hit me, lady. You can't just leave," the boomer man said.

Speaking again in Ivia, Paco said, "Spirit on Jacinto took him." Another guard arrived; they removed him from the gaming area.

Kaya would confront Andreas Alvarado. As she left, she heard the nice boomer lady who loved Mexican food say, "What kind of shitty casino is this? You better believe *we* won't be coming back to Palm Springs!"

■ ■ ■

One of the books Kaya read on business success for American women stressed the idea of being shrewd. She didn't possess this quality in any great abundance and was about to throw out everything she'd learned.

Andreas ordered the goon squad to leave his office and stand outside the door.

An eternity: They sat there, Andreas behind his desk, Kaya in front, staring each other down. The only sounds were the muffled dings and occasional shouts from the casino, footsteps in the hallway outside, the light hum of the air-conditioning when it kicked back in.

He hit his head on some rocks and he's dead. Paco's words hung in her mind like a broken record, repeating in an endless loop.

Andreas always looked bigger and meaner with that photo of him and that body-builder governor behind him on the wall. She assumed the placement was not an accident but carefully considered. "You make Jacy go up that mountain?" she asked.

His eyes narrowed. She could feel the heat and his hate for Jacy rise. "I heard what happened out there. I'm sorry. But guys like Jacy make their own luck, Kaya."

"No. You took advantage—you knew he'd do the things you could never do, and you really didn't care—"

"He had it coming!" Andreas picked up a little paperweight in the shape of Montana Grande and flung it past her head, hitting the opposite wall with a loud crack. "Jacy was with the Grecos, not with us, not with the tribe! Paco's right; the old spirits on that mountain took him."

So now he knows what he's long suspected, Kaya thought. Without another word, she got up. She would walk out of that office without running, and without looking back.

As soon as she slammed his door, the tears came. She'd make that fat fucker pay. She didn't know exactly how, but this was far from over.

■ ■ ■

Finally, Marina Boyko left Deepwell. She left with the odd pile of Pilar's clothing she was "taking to the dry cleaners" in the car that "wouldn't start." Sy realized he couldn't detain his lying maid without crossing a dangerous line, and he wasn't there yet. Not quite. He'd look around the house, see what he could find, try to contact his wife again.

His head still throbbed from whatever drug he'd been given. He stood at the refrigerator door, slurping milk out of the carton like a teenager. When he finished that, he started in on Pilar's iced tea. Yet everything moved in slow motion.

Sy shuffled back outside to check Candy again. She'd been shot; her blood was everywhere. He'd dialed 9-1 twice, already thinking better of pressing that third digit—perhaps it was best not to get the police involved until he knew more.

Another search of their bedroom turned up nothing except the obvious stripped mattress and box spring—even the plastic liners were gone. Marina *always* put fresh linens on the bed when she changed it; it was unheard of to see it like this, like someone was interrupted halfway through the task.

Everything else was as it should be and nothing looked out of place, just as he liked it. When he checked their home office, Pilar's laptop was gone, not unusual if she was working off-site, like she supposedly was. In Laguna. *Still* no answer to any of his texts or calls or emails.

Sy was struck with an overwhelming sense that he needed to get to the Greco office right away to check the safe. And who knew? Connor might be there. He covered Candy with a sofa throw. He'd take care of her later.

He drove past Greco & Greco twice and around the block before he parked on Tachevah, the side street.

Daniel was there, like always, looking good, like always. Sy sure knew how to pick employees. It didn't appear there was much of anything else going on, a normal day with Daniel sitting behind his desk.

"Morning, Dan—my wife here?"

Daniel rolled his chair back a few inches. "Everybody's looking for Mrs. G. today," he said. "She is one popular lady."

"What do you mean?"

Sy walked toward the office the Grecos shared. "Seems like every call that comes in is for her, and then one of the Mexican kids was here looking for her, too."

Mexican kid? That was half the staff. "Which kid are you talking about?" Her laptop wasn't on her desk here, either; not that he was surprised. "Has she called in at *all*?"

Daniel was in the doorway, arms crossed. He was the only guy Sy knew who'd wear a long-sleeve shirt in Palm Springs in August.

"You sick, Mr. G? You don't look so great. Mexican kid, Gomes. Hangs with Connor. That one."

Exactly right, not feeling good at all. He sat on his side of the huge U-shaped desk they shared. His back was sore from the night on the floor. "I didn't get much sleep."

The phone rang at Daniel's desk. He turned and skipped toward it. "Mrs. Greco is due at the end of the day, like always."

Sy heard Daniel's greeting, "Greco & Greco," which he likely repeated at least fifty times every day. He couldn't make out what came after that, but it didn't sound urgent or Daniel would've let him know.

Another wave of fatigue. Dehydration: He should drink something. Daniel usually filled the small kitchen in back with the carbonated water he liked and the expensive iced tea concoctions his wife demanded.

Sy walked past Daniel, who was now getting ready to leave. "An errand?" Sy asked.

Daniel sighed. He tossed his bag back on the desk. "You need me to stay?"

"I didn't mean that. Go ahead; I'll be here. I'll wait for Pilar."

Daniel left. When Sy returned from the kitchen with water he caught a glimpse of Daniel's red car turning out of the parking lot. He'd drop the water back at the big desk and check Daniel's work-crew lists, which were kept on a clipboard at reception. Those would show where Connor was supposed to be, also that "Mexican kid" George Gomes. Then he'd take a look at the safe, make sure the cash payoff was still in there.

He didn't make it that far. He woke—or came to—at his desk and only then realized he'd fallen asleep *again*. But it wasn't just that—it was noise; he heard footsteps, and that woke him. Someone was in the office.

■ ■ ■

Pilar didn't want her father inside her head today. What Rodrigo Galindez would think of Pilar Galindez Greco skulking back to Palm Springs to salvage what was left of a plan that turned out to be harebrained wasn't something she wanted to contemplate.

Or what he'd think of *any* plan to kill her husband, the father of her now dead son. So Angel didn't need a father around anymore; that was true. But Mr. Galindez liked Sy Greco for being Sy Greco. He was good at making money, he treated him with respect, but most of all he took Pilar out of Arizona. She was less of a distraction or disturbance. For that in particular, Sy always had value.

Why aren't these things ever easy? Sure wasn't like the movies she'd watched, *Double Indemnity* in particular. Pilar had never dreamed in a thousand nights that Connor would betray her. And with a Mexican *man*—if that wasn't somehow poetic, she didn't know what was.

What she wouldn't give to have seen the look on Connor's handsome face when he saw that the person that tool George killed wasn't Sy at all! She blushed, then giggled, catching herself in the rear view.

She'd figured correctly that Connor would be smart enough to remove the body; where to, she had no idea. Marina said there were no sheets on the Greco marital bed and there was nobody home. "Dead *or* alive, Mrs. Greco," she joked.

Pilar had passed Montana Grande's rival Morongo Casino and the tourist trap dinosaurs off Interstate 10, hurtling east toward Palm Springs. It had been only a couple of weeks since she'd met Nancy Argento under that stupid brontosaurus, but she'd turned out smarter than anybody realized, maybe even herself.

But now she had to hurry because things were beginning to come undone. Marina had called back to report a rumor, just as Pilar locked up the Laguna office. The desert maid network was reporting that an Indian kid had been killed on the mountain somehow, and that workers from Greco were involved.

This had to be a lie. Connor and his little Mexican toy had to be long gone, but he certainly couldn't be the only prize. If there was no cash to be had from a dead Sy Greco's will, they'd have a plan of their own, which Pilar would have to disrupt.

From down the block she could see the only vehicle parked near the office was one of their trucks—innocuous enough looking, but you never knew exactly who was driving what on any particular day, so there was no telling who was inside the office—if anybody. Midmorning was typically quiet there, as the crews were out and Daniel often ran errands.

Best to get in and get out; she'd worry about packing up the cash after she had it safely in her bag. It was still; there was no one in the front of the office, a warren of cubicles for their part-time agents as well as the main desk in front of the cacti—and the one plant that wasn't a plant.

Which she flew to as if it was her lover. Maybe it was—or what was inside was—since she didn't have Connor anymore, *the motherfucker.* The safe door, cut out of the stalk of the faux saguaro, fell open easily on her first try with her key and codes.

The cash drop from the tribe was still there. It looked huge.

"What the fuck is going on?"

Her bag was open and she hadn't put any money in it yet, so pulling her little baby Glock 9mm on Sy was easy.

"God, you scared me."

"Pilar—"

"You know what, Sy? I'm in charge here, so why don't *you* put this deposit in my bag?"

She stood and then he was on his knees, scooping stack after stack of twenties and fifties into her bag. Sy looked horrible. Passed out, drugged, on the floor overnight certainly didn't agree with him.

"Are you going to tell me why—"

"Shut up. Put it in there and I'm gone."

"Carrying this around, Pilar, is not going to be safe for you."

"I think *I* can decide what's safe for me and what's not."

The Gucci beach bag she'd brought—not small by any means—was nearly full. Did she have another one out in the car? She could kick herself.

"This money is half mine and you know it. My next call is to my friend the *police chief.*"

"Shut up. Those are *my* commissions. You never did anything to help sell a house. Just like you never helped take care of Angel when he needed it."

His face turned red and he threw the bag at her feet, hitting her ankle.

Her gun went off.

The bullet went through one of the real cactus plants, severing a branch.

Pilar screamed. "Fucking idiot!"

"Angel is better off dead than having a shit mother like you."

She kept her eyes on Sy as she grabbed the bag, pushing it behind her.

"This is my money and you know it. Hire a fucking lawyer; go ahead, you know them all. Now, get up."

Sy was on his hands and knees. Sweat dripped off his chin. "I'll find you. You know I will." He clutched the safe's open door to pull himself upright.

She felt sick, a giant headache descending. The office had a large supply closet in the center of the first floor. She'd lock Sy in there, buy herself some time.

She motioned the direction with the pistol. "Move."

He limped toward the hallway. Despite his lean physique, Sy wasn't a young man. "What did you do to my dog?"

"What are you talking about? Open that supply door and get inside."

He entered and she was right behind. She flicked on the overhead light. It was a small room with gray shelves along the walls, holding supplies like printer paper, open-house signs, Greco golf-cap promotions, that kind of thing. Most important, there was no phone in there. There was, however, a step stool.

"Candy's dead, a bloody mess by the side of the house. Someone shot her."

She wondered if he was lying, if he was testing her. Marina hadn't said a word about the Rottweiler.

"Sit." She waved the Glock at him and he complied. "You get what you want, Sy. This is your small payment for that. You can have that shit Connor—I suppose he'll eventually show up; he always does."

"Come on, Pilar. Don't do this. You'll never get away with it. You know it."

"Where's your phone?"

Sy patted his pockets front and back. "I don't have it; must be out in front or in the car."

"Turn out your pockets; let me see." He did as she asked.

Satisfied, she backed out the door and closed it, locking it. "We're a team. You're forgetting that," he said, though it came through muffled.

She pressed her forehead against the door. "I'm giving you another present. You won't have to worry about that nosy reporter Nancy anymore—that little Mex got rid of her."

The bag full of money was heavy. She had to drag it across the tile floor toward the door, doing her best to ignore Sy's nonstop, pathetic shouts from inside the closet. Then the office phone went off, ringing on a loudspeaker as it was supposed to do when no one was at the front desk, almost giving her a coronary. There was a message, also played over the PA system:

"This is Ted Ligett from the *Desert Sun*. Tracking down a colleague, Nancy Argento. Your office was in her log for this week. Please get back to me at—"

She didn't hear the number; the door had already closed behind her. She opened the trunk with her remote and gathered her strength to heave the money into it.

■ ■ ■

Lavender blinds were drawn down, though the slats were not completely closed. Diminished daylight filtered in; afternoon in the shadow of the mountain. An unseen television or radio was on, an RTE report in a heavy accent about the Irish government and their upcoming elections: A woman named Mona would not stop talking.

Connor's head felt like someone had taken a hammer to it. He thought if he opened his eyes the stimulation might be too much, might be the last light he ever saw. He lay on his back and he smelled two things: dust and pot.

Footsteps. He opened his eyes a tiny slit. The dust was from a desert trailer that was never cleaned. The pot came from Kevin, his silhouette moving down the narrow hallway, coming into focus as he walked toward Connor.

Kevin Kinsella, defrocked Irish nurse who lived in a creaky mobile home at the mountain end of Mesquite. Kevin was tall, skinny and pasty, never wore a shirt but always wore baggy floral drawstring pants, the kind you got at Phuket flea markets, four for ten bucks. He had an endless supply.

He exhaled marijuana over Connor. "You awake now, Connie? Wasn't sure I was ever gonna see those pretty blue eyes again."

Had he literally crawled up the steps to Kevin's trailer door and knocked on it, or was this a nightmare?

■ ■ ■

He'd been knocked out. The tram had just lurched forward on its long journey to the top of Jacinto and Jacy started a fight. That stupid Indian.

And they fell. God! Not the sensation of falling but of air; he remembered feeling the air rushing. Hot air. Then nothing. He heard gurgling, burbling. Water. Later, he came to lying at the base of one of the tamarisks lining the creek directly below the tram cables.

There was blood on his face—he could taste the iron—and excruciating pain coming from his shoulder and his left ankle.

And something else—rustling, panting, but not the human kind. Connor strangled out a horrified scream, loud enough so the coyote tugging at his pants leg backed off. It waited, looking stupid and primal, tight to the base of the tram support.

Through the tree branches above he could see enough in the predawn light that if the tram had been stuck above, it was gone now.

A more immediate concern was the coyotes. To Connor's left was Jacy, and he hadn't been so lucky. He'd fallen on boulders. His head was twisted toward Connor, lifeless eyes open, blood streaming in a trickle over the rock and down the sandy bank into the creek. Three coyotes waited a few feet away.

He had to get out of there and fast, but it was *so hard* to move. Connor pushed himself up with his left arm, the right one not wanting to work right. Something was wrong with his ankle—broken? sprained? He could limp or hop down to the parking lot; it wasn't that far. The limbs of the tamarisk had broken his fall but had also delivered some painful damage.

The wild dogs weren't used to people so they scattered back into the trees as soon as he stood. Connor easily found the old tribal pathway at the base of the canyon—the station was just through the trees and the parking lot right beyond that.

His heart sank when he hopped around the corner of the station and saw only one vehicle in the vast lot—Jacy's piece-of-shit car. Where was the Greco truck?

Where the fuck was George?

He could see the steel top arm of the tramcar sticking up out of the loading platform, so it was back down in the station berth. Climbing the ten steps up to take a look inside was pure torture, a little involuntary gasp each time he put some weight on his left foot and a sledgehammer of pain shot out the top of his skull.

All this while the desert sun snuck over the horizon to sear the land once more. He had to make it quick.

There wasn't much to see. George wasn't there. Nancy's body was gone. All the restaurant supplies—most of them anyway—were still loaded, the frozen food defrosted, leaking water out the open door.

He'd take Jacy's car. Connor's right arm and shoulder hurt so much he'd have to drive with one hand down the curving canyon road.

George must've thought the fall killed him. That was it, yes? The only explanation for why he'd left the mountain without looking for them. Pilar, too, would think this, once she heard about Jacy—which, with all her spies in town, would be soon.

Connor thought he heard something behind him just as he got to Jacy's car. A spark raced up his spine. He turned inch by inch, not only because it was so painful to move but also because he expected a reanimated, angry Jacy or another pack of coyotes.

Nothing was there; the sound was probably a rock falling off the cliffs, something that always happened on the mountain. It was just an empty landscape, beautiful in the increasing dawn despite what had happened.

If everyone assumed he was dead, Connor became part of that scene upon which anything—*anything*—could be written. Through his pain, he could already see this had advantages, even as he made his way back up to Jacy's body to get his keys.

10

Vi Gamble didn't like to have to look for a weapon. There'd been a time when she had a couple of guns—a pistol and a revolver, for variety—kept one in the silverware drawer in the kitchen and the other, always loaded, in her truck's glove compartment.

She got better at her job and as time went on there didn't seem to be any pushback from authority—or any trouble from competitors—so from time to time she "misplaced" them. They weren't exactly lost, but they most definitely were not in their assigned locations.

That was how she found herself in Duane's room. He'd been missing all week. God, what a freaking mess! This was nothing new: his filthy clothes, tools, dog-eared books from high school (*high school?*) scattered on the floor next to but not on a bookshelf, and dirt, the desert sand, which was supposed to stay outside. How it got in here was not a surprise, but this boy had not taken a broom to the floor in years.

Where would somebody like Duane keep his gun? He wasn't a person who hid much of anything, apparently, so it would likely be in plain sight. There was nothing like that here at all; he probably had it with him.

She hadn't seen him since Monday. He hadn't called; odd but not un-precedented. Unsettling. He'd get in these funks and go off into the desert or the mountains to blow off some steam.

Vi felt she needed to have a weapon handy because lately she'd been alone so much. Connor, living down in Palm Springs, pretending he was rich. Duane, God knows where. Locker, secretive, always kept things from her and his brothers, no change there except she knew in her bones something odd was up with him—more than the usual.

Or maybe it was the lines she'd put up her nose that made her so anxious. She caught herself in Duane's dresser mirror and laughed. She looked good, and she'd broken her own rule about not taking drugs when the big idea was to sell them and make a profit.

Vi didn't remember having the coke around; she found it in a routine check of her circuit of hiding places: behind sideboard drawers, in tissued shoeboxes on a shelf in her closet, even in that waterproof bag in the toilet tank at the back of the house. The coke—discovered in that rusty tank—was left over from a long-forgotten New Year's party when there wasn't much to celebrate, hence its continued existence.

So, one could say Vi Gamble was more energized on this particular day. Since she had no luck at all finding either a gun or any clue to Duane's whereabouts in his room, she moved on to Locker's.

As dirty and messy as Duane's room was, Locker's was the polar opposite, which she initially thought would make this task easier. Then again, moving objects in an already disorderly place would not arouse suspicion (at least not in Duane); the slightest alteration in the location of, say, a book or a T-shirt in her middle son's space was not advisable. He would notice. He would ask her why she'd been in his room.

But that would be later; she'd think of something. There was nothing out in the open. His laptop computer was closed, centered on the otherwise empty desk, its sides aligned parallel to the edges of the dark furniture. She wondered how it was possible she'd given birth to such a fastidious creature; she'd have to go into his drawers.

Which was where she found the papers.

The insane amount of real estate paper devoted to the sale of an old ice cream factory building down Highway 62. Purchased almost entirely *in cash*.

That was when Vi's brain scattered, like a completed jigsaw puzzle upended onto the floor, her eyes already wide and dilated but now scanning everywhere, unable to focus on any particular item in Locker's sterile room because the story she wanted to believe no longer matched the new evidence.

Hadn't Duane told her it was Locker—Locker and Connor who were skimming? Where else could this cash to buy property have come from? She took the sheaf of papers, tossing them onto her son's perfectly made bed.

Her red hair now damp against her temples, she went back to the desk, into the other drawers. She wasn't delicate or careful this time, not in the least concerned Locker would see something out of place and complain. Not now.

Finally, she found what she was looking for in his nightstand, so close to where he laid his precious dishonest head every night. It was time for some ice cream.

■ ■ ■

Vi turned off the highway, inched into the parking lot, thinking going slow on gravel would be less noisy, that nobody would hear her. She hadn't been able to resist doing another line before leaving home; her hands alternately gripped the steering wheel and shook.

Sure enough, here was Locker's car, the older Mercedes he'd repainted taupe, a camouflage color in the desert. Odd shade, come to think of it, since he liked flash, liked to stick out of the pack, liked criticizing little brother Duane in particular for his lack of style.

She thought the low building pathetic, though it was huge. The roofline gave the illusion it might collapse in on itself—or maybe that was really happening. She remembered the little ice cream retail joint tacked onto the edge. It looked different now. She'd taken the boys there when they were little, though they likely had forgotten that and the many other nice things their mother had done for them.

Now they wanted to take and take and take. *That stops right here,* she thought as she got out of the truck, still wearing the peach capris and old black flip-flops she'd had on in the house.

What would she say to him? Vi assumed Locker was alone in there, as his was the only car in the lot, though by itself that wasn't conclusive. And if there happened to be others with him in there, well—she'd brought protection.

The front door was unlocked, not odd in this corner of nowhere. Inside, it was mostly empty and dirty, what she would have expected. A pile of trash and building materials shoved off into one corner, a card table and folding chair under a translucent skylight that needed a major cleaning.

Small noises echoed off the rafters holding up the arched bow-and-truss roof. There was Locker, on his hands and knees in a corner, poring over blueprints. Plans that she had no knowledge of, plans that did not include her—yet were made possible because of *her* money.

Vi's face was hot. "Nice place you got here, son. These renovations must be costing a fortune."

His head jerked up as soon as she spoke. Slick as always, never missing a beat. "Been saving up, Ma. Locker's Garage. Like it?"

She walked toward him. "My ass! You've been stealing from me, from us, from your own brother. Nobody buys a building for cash."

He gathered up the plans, putting them in a stack behind him like he didn't want her to see.

"Connor makes a ton of money. Those Greco people are rich; you know that."

She was convinced they were alone. "Where's Duane? He hasn't been home for days."

Locker stood, brushing the dust off the knees of his lightweight chinos. "You know little bro. Probably in a tent somewhere."

She scanned the walls, the ceiling, the dirty skylight, back to the concrete floor. All of this paid for with her money, stolen by her own flesh and blood. She dug into her bag, slung over her shoulder, and took out the gun she'd found at home. Vi pointed it at Locker. "I can't believe you'd do this to me."

His jaw dropped, for once his smug façade showing a slight imperfection, a hint of fear. "Mom. What the fuck?"

"You'll sell this place; you'll give me my money back."

Locker threw his arms open. "But this *is* your money, right here! Doesn't matter where it came from. It's our ticket—Connor and me— away from *you* and all your skank dope!"

A cold slap to her face. She responded with an even colder pull on the trigger, unloading a bullet into his chest, the recoil knocking her back, the echoing bang in the empty factory deafening her. She watched him fall face-first onto that empty dusty floor, the blood radiating from under his shirt.

Locker tried to push himself up. It was impossible. He turned his head—odd, not even one hair out of place—with a look of confusion she knew so well. "It's all in . . . *Connor's* name, you stupid—"

He fell back down; he was quiet. She stood for a moment, forehead raised, listening: She heard nothing—no traffic, no wind, no nothing. Locker had found her a place in the middle of nowhere.

Vi Gamble hadn't gone there to kill Locker—really, she hadn't. It was the story she told herself; bad things happen sometimes. She didn't trust any of them, though—not her sons or their friends in the Marines or any of the others—so she needed a gun with her for protection. Anybody would understand this.

Now she needed to go find Connor. He'd also be her link to Duane; she was sure of it. A more immediate problem: What would she do with Locker? She couldn't just leave him there.

■ ■ ■

Jimbo McLaughlin's shoulder was sore from pressing too much weight. He always felt this first on turns, as in turning the steering wheel, which it seemed he did sixteen hours a day: drive here, drive there, drive everywhere. Before joining the Marines, he'd never thought he'd have a job where the same thing was repeated again and again without any deviation whatsover, but maybe that was the nature of jobs.

He could be so much more, but he didn't know how to do that, what steps he should take. That's what it was like being in a pair, which in his case meant being paired up with a psycho brother who looked exactly the same. They—Jimbo and Timbo—came as a package deal, and no options were considered that would break up this natural team.

Jimbo wanted out, even as he drove the Jeep with Timbo as his passenger on a quest to recover Duane Gamble's drug stash. He didn't like being thought of in the same breath as his brother, which had been inevitable throughout their shared twenty-three years. He didn't like what Timbo had become, and he was afraid of what he'd come to learn about himself.

But, then, looking at Timbo was like looking in the mirror, and they had such beauty now, it pleased him. Timbo's thick arms were like his own; didn't Jimbo love the way his own biceps would flex every time he negotiated a turn out of the base? He couldn't deny that, and he knew George admired him in that way. He'd seen him looking when he thought no one would notice. Jimbo did notice and felt that longing again. He'd tried so hard to ignore it, but with George it hit him like the Marine marching band.

If there was one thing in this world Timbo could never know, it was this. So in a way, it was good he'd turned into such a prick. Jimbo could erase him from his life for this reason and bypass the inevitable rejection for liking men.

They'd entered the dusty subdivision in Yucca Valley where Vi and Duane lived and were almost on top of the Anaconda Lane turn. Timbo put up his hand. "Slow down; pull over here, Jimmy. Let's make sure she's not home."

Jimbo fished his disposable phone out of his back pocket and dialed the number. Like he expected, Vi's screechy greeting admonished him to leave a message, which he did not do. He disconnected, then tossed it onto the seat next to Timbo.

All clear.

For reasons Jimbo did not know and did not ask about, Timbo had a key to Vi's back door. They went in. The kitchen was spooky quiet, raising the light hair on the back of Jimbo's neck. There was the smell of stale coffee from a cold aluminum pot on the counter. Next to it sat a wrinkled tomato where a small patch of white mold grew. He'd never been here when the Gambles weren't home. Duane was still missing; no one knew where he'd gone. For sure he took the drugs with him—*right?*—a no-brainer.

Timbo stopped at the dark hallway that led to the rest of the house. Above him, an air-conditioning vent hummed to life, the cool breeze tumbling down.

"Let's split—you go to Duane's room; I'll see what's down here," he said, disappearing into the messy living room where the sun struggled to get through gaps in Vi's old curtains. "If I was an idiot like Duane Gamble, where would I put my drugs?"

Jimbo passed the room he figured was Locker's—the only way he could be sure was because of the clothing on display: The closet door was open, and Locker had so many club shirts he'd hung the overflow on a makeshift vinyl clothesline attached to a curtain rod. Yet it wasn't orderly like you'd expect from someone so anal. The mess reminded Jimbo of a horny teenager's lair.

He didn't go in, continuing as directed to Duane's room at the end of the hall. If Locker's room was in slight disarray, it was like an explosion had hit this one. Someone had already been in here looking.

If this were my room, where would I hide bags?

One thing Marines had in spades was boots. Both he and Timbo often hid drugs and cash and the occasional firearm in standard-issue footwear. He'd start with the closet; surely there'd be shoes in there.

He didn't remember Duane as a rider, but there was a pair of mid-calf boots stuck way in back. Jimbo grabbed the pair and shook them out, though the only treasure was one dead cricket.

Same with the other shoes, without even the bugs. He checked boxes, old suitcases, backpacks, and came up with nada. In drug dealer terms, what Duane owed the twins was hardly worth this kind of effort. Just as it seemed like he'd never find anything, Jimbo slid his knee along a floor-board that gave a little.

In a desert tract house like Vi's, the usual flooring of whatever nature was right on top of a concrete pad. Under that were only dirt, bedrock and China. Or so one would think.

It didn't take much prying to get the floorboard to slide out, and there it was, small plastic bags filled with pills packed together. He took one packet out of the cubby; it appeared Duane had a previously unknown stash of meth.

"You found it, Jimmy, good job." Timbo stood in the doorway. It was like looking in a full-length mirror, one that was always a surprise and you'd rather not see.

The two of them loaded their booty into one of Duane's old back-packs and placed it between them on the Jeep's seat. Jimbo anticipated more big drama when Duane eventually found out his drugs were gone, and he'd figure out pretty quick who took them.

Jimbo no longer wanted any part of it. "Timmy, these are yours," he said. "You and Manny up at the base can work this game alone. I'm out."

"No, no, Jim. You can't ever be really *out*. Doesn't work that way."

■ ■ ■

Eventually Sy, still stuck in the closet, had to pee. All the cursing and screaming of Pilar's wretched name hadn't done him any good, hadn't elicited any kind of response whatsoever. That was the trouble with the desert in August—everyone fled. They'd find him for sure, but it would first take an afternoon spent alone in a windowless room.

Lucky for him, there were a few leftover Greco-branded golf tourna-ment water cups stacked on a shelf. So far he'd used two—pissed in them, then placed them in a row along the corner against the wall, covering both with a fresh legal pad. It still smelled like urine. He was reasonably certain he would't have to take a shit in there, but if he did, that would only be added to the already good reasons to destroy Pilar and Connor.

Unless he got out of there soon, she'd be long gone with that money. Knowing Pilar, she'd head south, probably to Mexico, unless she thought he'd go looking for her in places they'd visited often, like Vallarta or Ajijic. But she wouldn't drive over the border with the cash.

Connor was the unknown, the wild card. Sy had time to reflect on that as he waited for the minutes, these interminable hours, to tick down to seven P.M., when, if he remembered correctly, the cleaning crew arrived.

Sy had not been as shrewd as he normally would be, where Connor Hurst was concerned. He could have seen this coming: Some kid with Connor's looks and charm and, yes, even brains would in time hatch a plan to fucking rob him blind.

And why shouldn't he be bisexual, too? Hello, look in the mirror; this really happens, and even if it's rare, it sure happened here with Connor and Pilar. Sy picked up a ream of copy paper and hurled it at the door, where it bounced with a dull thud before landing back at his feet.

Nobody will hear this but you.

That's it, get the anger out; his therapist (suggested by Pilar, after Angel's accident) always reminded him that keeping his feelings bottled up wasn't a good strategy. So this was a start, though he couldn't let this overshadow what was best for the business. Damage control was what it would all be about. Get rid of Connor, easy, then Pilar, not so easy, or perhaps easy but not inexpensive. Then go on like before. Nothing else had changed, right?

But he had to get out. He'd seen enough movies where spies or detectives or criminals had picked or jimmied locks and doorknobs. He was in an office supply room—there *had* to be something he could MacGyver to get that door open.

Lots of pens, too thick to fit in any keyhole. Paper clips were what he tried to find; wasn't that what they always used? Simply unravel the wire, stick it in the lock and then presto, *click*, you were out.

Except that both of the Grecos had emphasized paperless and virtual office agendas for their company, one of the goals being to save on supplies. So they didn't have cartons of things like paper clips. They'd likely have a tiny box or two, and they'd be here in the supply room only if some-one hadn't appropriated them.

Eventually he located two small boxes of clips on the shelf above his urine depository: One contained the newer plastic variety, in red, which did not unravel into a thin wire at all. The other box had possibilities.

He sat on a large plastic tub, wall paint leftover from an upgrade ear-lier in the year. Breathing in what was rapidly becoming his own rank body odor, Sy realized he hadn't taken a shower in days and this was the second night he'd sleep in these clothes, if he didn't get out.

He pushed and pulled and twisted the paper clip wire in the lock, but he didn't know what he was doing and nothing happened, nothing worked—this was not the movies. Tiredness again fell like a thunderclap, a trace of those drugs still in his system. He'd lie down, for only a few minutes, in the cool right in front of the door so he'd hear when someone came in the building at last and he could call out.

Sy didn't know how long he'd been out when he heard a key turn in a much bigger lock and a whoosh of air being sucked in as the front door opened.

"This is what being dead must be like," he whispered, half-dreaming. Then he pressed his cheek to the cold floor and bellowed: "I'm locked in this closet! Open the fucking door!"

■ ■ ■

It turned out not to be the cleaning crew at all, but Daniel Pearson him-self, come back to work from errands because tomorrow was going to be "a day from hell, Mr. G."

A day from hell for the various agents with open houses, those trying to close deals in August—a good month for desert bargains—and as the sole admin, Daniel's plate was "always on overflow, Mr. G."

It occurred to Sy—however fleetingly, as he knew this was not how these things worked—how more beneficial it would've been to have had an affair with the blond and willowy Daniel, who was gay, not bisexual in any way, and eminently trustworthy. If Daniel were a 10 on the honesty scale, Connor Hurst would come in at about 4.5.

But, of course, this was definitely not how things worked. Daniel brewed coffee while Sy washed up in the men's room and tried out several lies in his head. Not that it really mattered. Daniel was the type to outwardly accept anything a Greco might say, however dishonest or ludicrous it might sound. What he was thinking inside was most days inscrutable.

Daniel had asked, "What happened?"

Sy answered, "I got locked in the closet by mistake."

The admin's eyes widened but he had tasks to perform. He looked to the floor for a moment, then went to the windows to close the blinds against the setting sun. "Fresh coffee will be ready in a few minutes," he said.

Sy returned from the restroom with a small towel draped over his shoulders. "Whoever closed up earlier did not realize I was in the supply room," he said. "And as luck would have it, I left my phone in the car."

"Should I call Mrs. G?" Daniel consulted the online calendar on his computer screen. "I've still got her down to be back from Laguna by the end of the day." He made a few clicks into his email. "Weird, no messages from her this afternoon. Must be busy down there."

"No, no, *no*; don't call her; let's not bother her. To be honest, I'm a little embarrassed I got myself all messed up like this. But you know, who I *do* need to find is Connor, and that Spanish kid you were talking about before, that one who calls himself George."

Daniel took a sip out of his hot beverage cup and sat at the desk. A few clicks on the keyboard later: "Looks like Connor is off today. And George—right, he was here earlier, asked where we needed a crew member, asked to see Mrs. G. But, Mr. G, I forgot to tell you; he works part-time now at that gay bar on Arenas, the dance bar. He might be there in the afternoons, but I'm not sure." He stood up and smiled. "You don't really trust him, *do you*, Mr. G?"

■ ■ ■

Sometimes "his" Southridge mansion was too quiet even for George Gomes. He'd been back off that mountain now for twelve hours, a little more. If he stayed here at his isolated, deserted and enormous home, he might pretend nothing at all had happened, that all was still right in Connor's world, in Nancy Argento's world. In his own world even, where he'd started to really believe his name was George, and he could be . . . British or a rich guy from Polanco or something like that.

Seemed like he spent interminable hours sitting on the lip of this pool, his feet dangling in the water kicking back and forth. He'd been a bad brother, hadn't he? Not one pool party for the boys, Jesse and Chuy, no water guns, no Marco, no Polo. Now it would never happen. With Connor gone, it was only a matter of time—and not much of that at all—before they'd come and he'd have to find another place.

George had to admit the lack of furniture inside the house had begun to creep him out. Onto the vast and empty white walls he could project any scene; often these were images he wanted to go back and change: that night with Jacy at Ralph's; the time he didn't fight off Sy; watching Connor fall out the open door of the tram.

Useless daydreaming. It was best to move on, carry out the rest of the plan. *Es la vida,* Alma Gomez might say. She occasionally came up with things like this in great solemnity, universal truths applied to any situation that defied easy explanation.

He couldn't wait much longer—he needed to get back to the Greco office and then get away. It was nearing the end of the workday, but if Daniel was still there, he'd have to take care of that. Do whatever was necessary to get into that safe.

George paced the house, thought there was good evidence he was, in fact, going crazy, losing it. Alongside the pool, in back through the doors, past the empty family room, through to the grand and empty living room and entrance hall, where he could see the street, where he could check traffic, such as it was. If he needed protection, the guns from the night before were back in the utility closet by the pool.

But there wasn't much traffic. August in the desert, people who could afford these homes had places in other climates; they weren't crazy and they were rich. So when George saw the shirtless figure of Jimbo the Marine walking up the driveway to the door, he was in rights to think, at first anyway, it was a hallucination, a mirage.

He told George that he was through with his brother—it was like looking into a lying mirror every day. After Timbo and he moved all Duane's stash out of the Jeep, Jimbo left his brother and drove west along Twentynine Palms Highway. He knew where he had to go, whom he had to see—and it was George. Jimbo took the highway all the way down into Palm Springs then drove up the hill to the mansion where he knew George would be.

Any guilt he might have felt for what had happened to Connor evaporated when George sank into Jimbo's strong arms. "I had to see you," the soldier said.

They fell into the bed at the back of the house. The sex was quick and rough, seemed like Jimbo had to be relieved of something deeper than mere desire for George. Being smaller than most guys, George was comfortable taking the more submissive role again with Jimbo, as he knew how much this pleased Connor.

He'd figured out that the one desired that way ends up being the one in control, which was really where George increasingly found himself. He liked it. He liked being in charge—back at the trailer in Mecca, during what had always seemed his endless horrible life, this wasn't anything he'd ever considered. Power could be had if a guy was smart enough to take it.

Jimbo would be his new love. They lay there, in sweat, staring at the ceiling, though George knew their time in the house was just about over. His head lay on Jimbo's big arm. He had to tell.

"Connor is dead, Jimmy."

Jimbo turned his head and grinned at George. "Shhh, *papi*, time for my nap."

"He fell out of the tram. In a fight, with Jacy! He's dead on that mountain over there. So is Jacy."

Jimbo sat up. "What are you talking about?"

George didn't know how much he should tell Jimbo about the plan—that plan to kill Sy—that plan that went so bad. He blurted some of it out, like the part about Nancy Argento—it was an accident!—they found this lady dead, dead in a bed.

But they had to get rid of her, so Connor insisted on taking her up the mountain. It was all his idea, it was all *his* fault. George wasn't even sure if Jimbo knew who Nancy was, so he likely wouldn't care. He'd been to war. Dead bodies were nothing new to a man like him.

Jimbo was telling George, "Actually, man, you don't look so good," when they both heard a screaming car motor abruptly cut off, right outside the front door. George wasn't at all surprised. He knew someone would come.

11

Dios! Sy.

George caught a glimpse of the older man through the window, while Jimbo hopped around the bedroom on one foot struggling to get his camo pants back on. It was easy to figure this out; he had come in an official Greco & Greco truck, now parked right behind the one George had "borrowed." It also made sense it would be Sy, owner, leader of the pack, who'd be most outraged at the little brown squatter in his midst.

But then it wasn't just Sy by himself. He didn't arrive empty-handed. George's jaw dropped as Sy grabbed a shotgun sitting next to him on the passenger seat just as he opened the truck's door.

"Jimbo! Where's the Jeep?" George shouted back to the bedroom, his raised voice echoing off the white walls of the empty house. Wearing just his T-shirt, he sprinted to the front door, bolted it and locked the doorknob as well, hoping to buy them a few minutes. "I'm blocked in."

He didn't think Sy would damage a house he'd almost completely fixed up—he wouldn't want to have to pay for a new door. Among other things. But George didn't want to take any chances. Jimbo tossed him his jeans, which had been thrown at the foot of the mattress an hour or so before. "I parked on the street. We'll go over the wall out back and come around."

Sy banged on the front door. His voice, though muffled by the thick wood, was strangled like nothing George had ever heard out of him before.

They had to run. George could come back later to retrieve whatever clothing and personal items he left behind.

Sy kicked at the door. Maybe he didn't give a fuck about having to replace it. He punched the doorbell over and over, sending a unending, deafening church chime echo through the rooms.

"Can't we just see what he wants?" Jimbo had seemed so smart. Now he asked stupid questions that would only delay their exit.

No. We can't see what he wants. I know what he wants; that's why we're running, mister! Jimbo and George had slid around a corner of the house when they heard an enormous crash—Sy had either broken down the door or shot it open. They weren't going to stop to find out which.

"Where do I go?" Jimbo shouted over the start-up warning bells, country music radio and engine roar of his jeep.

"Away—downhill—get off this hill."

The Jeep lurched from the curb, Jimbo taking the first switchback turn with relative ease.

But not before George turned around to see Sy run back out the front door to the company truck he came in. He was coming after them.

It was one of those late afternoon summer Thursdays when those fools who stayed in the desert all year long were out of their caves doing errands, many heading to the weekly street fair. So—there was a bit of traffic. Maddeningly slow traffic. George thought it might produce cover, a distraction—and they could lose Sy.

He didn't dare look again till they'd gotten off the hill and crossed over East Palm Canyon. Jimbo was headed north on Gene Autry Trail out into the desert, picking up some speed while an Alaska Airlines 737 thundered above them, swooping in for a landing at the neighboring airport.

The roar and vibration of the jetliner made George tremble. So he turned. Sure enough, the Greco truck with Sy at the wheel was behind them, one car in between.

His head spun. Should he tell Jimbo more? About the money? No, no, no! Sy didn't even know about that. How could he? He was after Connor. George couldn't very well admit he'd left Connor on a mountain to die—he'd have to tell the whole story and that was not an option.

"God, where do I go? He's gonna catch up," Jimbo cried.

They had about run out of city and were heading past big vacant lots loaded with sun-blasted trailers parked on cracked concrete pads, beyond which was empty desert and the looming windmill farm.

Jimbo took a gamble and turned off onto an unmarked street leading into the sand, hoping for a shortcut back to Highway 111. Then he'd circle back to town and lose the old man in the chaotic street-fair jam.

But Sy was right on his bumper, leaning on his horn.

That was a funny thing about Palm Springs—in minutes you could be in the middle of nowhere with no one around for what seemed like miles, even if it was a mirage. What loomed ahead of them was no illusion, however.

"Oh, fuck, look, George—I have to stop."

A low stone wall, vestige of something left over from the early twentieth century when someone tried to turn Palm Springs into farms, blocked any further ingress into the desert. The crumbling blacktop didn't end; it made a ninety-degree exit to the left to a turnaround circle in the sand.

There was literally nowhere they could go.

"Sorry. Guess that turn was not my best move."

George didn't respond, his head filled with images of the family trailer in Mecca, the Homeland Security bus with the barred windows rolling up to the border at Calexico.

And there was Sy, caught up to them, grinding to a halt in a sickly brown cloud of dusty sand, an enormous windmill revolving slowly above them.

Jimbo cocked his head at George. "Now you're going to see a real Marine." He jumped out of the Jeep and with what could be described as a bull charge toward Sy, he let out a high-pitched shriek.

Sy stood next to his pickup. Maybe it was the reduced visibility from the dust, or maybe Jimbo was simply not the best Marine, but he—or his head—ran directly into the butt of Sy's shotgun.

He fell to the dirt, out cold.

Sy looked as surprised as George felt. He jumped out of the Jeep and ran to Jimbo—who moaned, though he was hard to hear above the constant, unnerving white noise of desert wind.

George tapped Jimbo's cheeks. His eyes opened.

"He'll be OK, *Jorge*." Sy raised his rifle again, pointing it at George. "All I want from you is that thief Connor."

George put his palm under Jim's head and lifted it an inch off the sand. "I don't know nothing about him and I don't think you're gonna see Connor ever—"

Something moved in the low brush next to Sy. He didn't see it as quickly as George did. Then he jumped.

Rattlesnake.

In that blink, George dropped Jimbo back into the dirt and rushed Sy. He tried grabbing the shotgun, but Sy, far larger, hit him and George fell—though close enough to Sy to grab his leg, upsetting his balance.

Sy lost his grip on the gun and it fell onto the hard sand. Just a couple of feet away from the rattler now, they fought to grab the rifle first. Quicker, George won. He stood, backed up a foot and aimed it at Sy.

Jimbo sat up. "Fuck, my head—"

Sy put his hands up. "Please, Jorge—don't do anything foolish. Let's work through this."

George had—perhaps—fired a long gun like this a couple of times, years ago in Mexico, then again at Vi's. He sure would hit *something*.

"Stupid man. Look at me. I don't have any Connor here, just look!"

The snake moved closer to Sy's foot. "I'm going to take a step to my right; don't fucking shoot me," he said.

"Get back in that truck and go," George said. "I'll keep your nice gun. Keep going; don't come back—I'll use it. I promise I'll use it."

Sy squinted at the two younger men. "Now, look—"

"Get in that car and drive and don't stop until you get to fucking Florida!"

He stood there, stupidly, his hands up still. Jimbo got to his feet, wobbling, the heel of his palm pressed on his forehead to stanch the bleeding. "You heard the man," he said.

Glancing down first—the snake had slithered out of sight—Sy backed toward his truck. Overhead, the eerie, metronomic *whomp-whomp-whomp* of the windmill punctuated his moves.

"Hurry up. Get in there and drive," George said. He pointed the shotgun to the left of the truck and blasted a prickly pear, making Sy and Jimbo jump. The cactus exploded, bits of it dripping off the truck's Greco & Greco lettering.

Sy started up the engine and drove away with such care it was as if he was worried about running over that snake. George and Jimbo watched, enveloped in the dust the tires kicked up.

"How's your head, Jimmy?"

"He'll be back and he won't be alone," Jimbo said.

■ ■ ■

Pilar Greco hated Thursdays. Because of the weekly street fair, inevitably she'd get stuck in horrid tourist traffic going home. Still, she was happy with the quieter location chosen for the Greco & Greco offices—North Palm Canyon—where there were no late-night businesses, no restaurants, no bars, no hotels, even, with noisy midnight stragglers from Los Angeles pulling in off Highway 111.

When they were looking for office space years before, Sy had argued for something closer to the building trades, the hardware and interior-decorating locations at the south end of Palm Springs—*Also, it's closer to home, honey*—but she deemed the storefronts available not elegant enough and she was right. Their office was as quiet as a tomb, even if on this particular evening one of the partners was locked up in an interior storeroom.

Back home, she'd poured herself some of that special Black Maple Hill whiskey, choosing a fresh, unopened bottle, as even though no one ever spiked the one meant for Sy, you couldn't be too careful. People forget what they do, all the time.

The sheets on their bed were missing, as was Nancy Argento's body, of course. Curious—there was no blood; chalk that up to the miracle of modern plastic. That cover was likely now wherever Nancy was. Maybe that was where Candy was as well, as she sure wasn't anywhere outside. *Marina is an angel, an angel with a sword.*

Pilar shivered, dripping whiskey on the floor, just missing her still open suitcase. But what she wouldn't give for a photo of Connor's face when he realized Nancy was not Sy!

She tried to remember Montevideo as the opposite, that it was winter there, so pack the heavier clothes. *Quickly, quickly, quickly!* She caught herself in the bedroom mirror, holding the drink. Her brown eyes were a little puffy—that lack of sleep. Behind her on the mattress were the two olive leather bags, almost full. On the floor was the shipping box where she'd packed the money, nearly three hundred thousand dollars.

Which was only a fraction of what it should have been. Somehow, Connor must have taken the rest. She didn't know how, but she'd figure it out and come up with a plan to get it back. It would be night soon. She had to take that box out to the shipping place in Palm Desert and send it to herself.

Pilar squeezed her eyes shut and downed the rest of the whiskey. After that, she'd get right to the airport for her flight to Houston: the gateway to South America.

Sy would chase her first to Scottsdale, and then he'd assume, since Pilar had no contact with her parents, that she'd gone to Mexico, to see her expat college girlfriends in Ajijic. He'd never guess Montevideo or even one of those Italian towns in southern Brazil. She hadn't made up her mind. The money would go far in either place.

Get me out of here. Pilar was hyperaware of the impairment alcohol could cause, and the last thing she'd ever be compared to would be that insect who killed Angel. Still, there were those special occasions, like this one. Liberation, independence: even a pleasant silver lining to the Connor betrayal.

None of that changed that this was a long drive down valley; darkness was closing in fast; it would be fully dark when she arrived. She had to hurry. The highway patrol often set up sobriety checkpoints along this road, but in summer the pickings were slim and it wasn't worth their while.

As she rounded a curve in Rancho Mirage and hurtled toward the long, almost imperceptible decline into Palm Desert, she could see the distant stoplights where she'd turn into the parking lot. She relaxed her clenched midsection and let out a grateful exhale.

The quiet monotone of the local radio station soothed her; the weather report, clear and hot, was as normal as it was advantageous for on-time departures. This would work. Greco & Greco had routinely shipped international documents to Uruguay a number of times in the past year; packages were never opened and there'd never been a delay.

The shipping office was the only storefront with all its interior lights still ablaze.

She shouldn't have worn low pumps; it was complicated enough to get the box out of the trunk and carry it inside. Negotiating the airport would be worse, yet these uncomfortable Louis Vuittons were made for the TSA.

At the door, Pilar dropped the package on the concrete and was going to hold the entrance open with her foot. The door opened as if by magic, sending a wave of panic through her. She thought for a second she would vomit.

Someone was holding the door for her, a young man, smiling down. No one she knew. He wore a dark blue shirt, company logo. "I've got it, miss," he said. "Let me help you with that."

Pilar drew in a sharp breath, her heart pounding against her ribs. "That's all right. I can manage—but thank you. Thanks."

He was Latino, pretty much like everyone who had this kind of job in the desert, and must have been really young, as his attempt at a beard could be thought of as endearing if it weren't so pathetic. Still, he was handsome and she appreciated the interest.

"If you're sure," he said. "It's still so hot out here."

She picked up the box and held her breath for the ten or so paces it took to place it on the shipping counter.

The boy who'd held the door disappeared into the back, where they made copies and collated booklets. The other employee, a middle-aged woman with hair the slutty color Pilar always thought of as "Summerlin red," took a look at the address she had written on the box and pulled the appropriate forms from their bins.

"Honey, for international you need to fill these out," she said, her eyes heavy lidded with a shadow underneath; it didn't appear working days agreed with her. "What's in the box?"

Another wave of nausea enveloped Pilar. She pressed her left palm against her stomach. "Documents, like always. Seems we're forever sending real estate prospectuses to Montevideo."

"So—no need for insurance?"

"Not this time."

The clerk nodded, put a pen on the counter, and turned back to a box she was in the middle of packing: a granny's old English floral china collection.

Pilar felt warm air at her back, a summer desert hazard meaning the door to the outside was open; someone was letting in the heat. She was about to turn when she felt a familiar, strong hand on her shoulder.

Oh fucking God! It was Connor.

"I thought you—"

"Whatever you thought, I guess you were wrong."

He had a long scrape down his cheek, freshly scabbed. He, too, looked like he hadn't slept well. His tan slacks were soiled, odd for someone so fastidious. There was a hole near the bottom of his aqua T-shirt. His hair was dirty.

"What's in the box, Pilar?"

She would do her best to ignore this situation—there were two employees, maybe more; Connor was outnumbered and it wouldn't take her but a couple more minutes.

"I'm not going to ask what happened to you, because *I really don't care.*" She glanced at her watch; two hours and she'd be on that plane to Houston. She had to move.

"He'll find you," Connor whispered. "Sy's already looking, I know it."

The boy in the blue shirt joined his coworker behind the counter. "Is there a problem, miss?" he asked, as Pilar hesitated.

Connor stepped back, resting a hand on an adjacent counter. She realized he was injured, unsteady, more than was readily apparent.

"We're fine," she said to him, putting on her finest real estate saleslady smile, the sincere one. She turned to Connor. "Funny, I'm not that worried about Sy. You were stalking me at Deepwell?"

Pilar knew that before she left this office her package would be on its way out of the country. Then she could relax, begin to pick up the rest of the disarray from the past couple of days. Even figure out what to tell herself about Nancy Argento.

Connor grabbed her wrist and twisted it, making her shriek.

"Half of that's mine!" he shouted. He pushed her out of the way and lunged at the counter, grabbing the box from Summerlin Red, who hadn't finished taping on the various international shipping stickers.

Startled, she jumped back, allowing Connor to pull the box off the counter.

"No!"

Pilar brought her fist down on his back, hitting a shoulder blade, not stopping him in the least.

He half ran, half limped to the door.

She came around his side, grabbed a corner of the box, tried to pull it away. One of her nails came off. Connor used the weight of the package to push her back as he backed into the door handle.

Pilar lost her balance and fell on her ass, hitting the hard floor. Connor was out the door, in the parking lot, getting into a beat-up car she didn't recognize.

"Stop him! That fucking *thief*! Help me, *please!*"

The Latino kid and Summerlin Red stood there, mouths open, safely behind their counter barrier.

"Honey, you want us to call the police?" Red asked.

■ ■ ■

Jesse and Chuy Gomez weren't twins, though well-meaning but ultimately stupid adults often thought so. They were stupid because any idiot could see that Jesse at eight was at least an inch taller than Chuy at seven at any given time, though both *chicos* were growing fast.

George (or Jorge, as he was still known in the trailer) observed that indeed, this was harder to realize when the boys were sitting, as they happened to be, right across from him, unenthusiastically eating Alma Gomez's rice and beans.

As was Jorge Gomez, or George Gomes, though George really did now prefer the more Americanized food Connor Hurst had introduced him to, for instance, those crunchy yogurt and granola parfaits—for breakfast—maybe with an egg, too. With no tortillas in sight.

A long weekend had now passed since the nightmare on the tram and the fight with Sy. George had been too afraid to return to the house on the hill— *"his" house*—to get what few items he'd left there, most of which were Greco work clothes. Jimbo had done a drive-by, reported that crews were back at work up there. They likely threw everything out—probably thought it was the refuse of a squatter, perhaps some homeless wreck of a person who broke in.

George didn't like being back at the trailer in Mecca, and he didn't like eating his mother's food. This was all temporary. And it went without saying, though it gave him a shiver whenever he thought about it—it was a damn good thing he hadn't stashed any of the Greco money he took anywhere in that Southridge house.

No, his several visits to "Danny's prickly pear"—started back when he'd had to do that first bank deposit for Pilar—had been more rewarding than even he was hoping, uncounted cash on its way to or from the casino, sometimes even unbundled.

The years of hiding his gay porn magazines under his mattress shoved to the far edge of the trailer wall reinforced the idea that this was, actually, a great hiding place. Never once in all those years had Alma Gomez or the two younger brothers suspected anything was hidden there.

This time it had been more of an investment, however. George cut a hole in the old box spring, mostly hollow anyway and a perfect receptacle for cash. He knew he couldn't leave it there for long—someone would find it eventually, the piece-of-shit trailer would burn, or there'd be some other catastrophe he hadn't thought of yet.

And that could be Connor, of course. He seemed to have evaporated from the planet. George played it over and over in his head: He *had* seen Connor and Jacy fight; he had seen Jacy fall out the tram door and take Connor with him. It was he who had pushed Nancy Argento's body off the tram farther up the mountain, no doubt providing breakfast for Jacinto coyotes, then maneuevered the tramcar by trial and error back down to the mountain station.

He learned two things from this: (a) Any idiot could operate that tram-car, and (b) he, George Gomes, could operate without Connor.

Local news reports and conventional wisdom determined that Jacy's death was an accident. Who cared anyway? Since that park was adminis-tered by the tribe, it was really no business of the normal powers that be in Palm Springs. As far as George knew, no one was looking into it further.

So far, anyway, so good. At least on Jacy. But it was only his body the news ever talked about; they'd found only one body on the mountain un-der the tram.

So what had happened to Connor?

He'd get out of this hellhole in maybe another week at most; he needed a few more days of calm to let things settle. Sy had either left town as instructed or was lying low—George didn't know for sure, but he didn't expect the older man would be gone forever. When he finally returned, things would explode.

So he couldn't be here; he couldn't be the one to lead Sy or even Pilar to his little brothers or his mother, who usually meant well, though clue-less was so often her working method.

Case in point: the air conditioner, one of those cheap models they roll out the door of big-box stores by the dozens, easily replaced. The current one in the trailer wall was broken—OK, it worked at a base level, its hum straining to push out even a tiny stream of cool air. It wasn't like she didn't have the money; he'd been giving her a portion of his Greco pay all along.

So it was sweltering at the breakfast table, as early as it was, the sun barely over the hills to the east. Jorge winked at Chuy, his little mouth full of tortilla, sitting there shirtless with his brother, both of their chests as flat as boards, skinny brown kids with their ribs sticking out.

Alma appeared back at the table holding her smoking frying pan, dishing out a single fried egg to each of the boys, including one for Jorge. The burned lard made him gag, which made Chuy giggle, which made him spit out the half-chewed food onto his plate.

"*Mijo!* That is disgusting!" his mother cried, tapping his head with her dripping fork.

Both George and Jesse laughed.

"This is not funny," Alma said. "You never get anywhere in this life without manners. Eat with your mouth closed."

"That's right, boys, eat this nice breakfast your mama made for you," George said. Alma leaned in to kiss him. She lifted the chain of the silver and turquoise pendant that hung around his neck. "Where did this come from?"

"My boss at Grecos, a guy, Connor, he gave it to me."

She returned to the stove and dropped the iron frying pan onto the dirty grate. "Jorge, I don't like seeing this kind of thing on you. It's what the *maricones* wear."

Jesse and Chuy looked at him wide-eyed. George's face turned hot. "I'll wear what I fucking like," he said, pushing his plate to the table edge.

■ ■ ■

George wouldn't stay where he wasn't wanted. It was night now; he lay there under a thin sheet, naked on his mattress, the only thing moving the still searing air from an old fan he found next to the trailer community trash dump.

He was on his back, knowing that a few inches under his ass was the money that would allow escape, anytime. Next to him, Jesse snorted and turned in his lower position on the boys' bunk beds. George didn't want to leave them alone with Alma, but he knew that down the road this money would help all of them.

Maybe that time was now. The sooner he left, the quicker their lives would be better.

He realized there was no way he could go back to Greco & Greco, check out that cactus to see about more goodies. They'd be waiting for that; the first thing the Grecos would have done anyway was to take away any remaining cash. George would have to accept that what he had was going to be it, and be grateful for it.

Over the white noise of the fan, he heard something else, not one of the boys making sounds in his sleep, but something outside the trailer. It wasn't that unusual; people who lived here came and went at all hours and the trailers themselves were disconcertingly close to one another. Still, it *was* the middle of the night.

He stood to peer through the blinds at the window right above his bed. No one was there; streaks of greenish light from the park lamp made the other trailers and their shadows look like bunkers in an abandoned prison camp.

The rustling continued—an animal, probably, in the oleander that separated their little "yard"—if you could call it that—from the property boundary, beyond which was a vacant desert lot. George pulled on his shorts and went to the door.

His heart pounded against his chest. Except for Connor, no one from Greco knew exactly where he lived or was from; he'd kept that vague: *East valley, it's all the same, poor and mean and I'm so happy I'm not there.* Nor would they be likely to find him. None of these trailers had numbers. The post office drove by the main gate without stopping and tossed the bag of mail over the fence, trusting management to deliver it to residents—which sometimes even happened.

He couldn't go back to bed. Pulling the front door sharply to the right before opening it—to avoid the horrible, noisy "stick" it had and waking Alma or the boys—George stepped outside, where it was still mid-80s yet felt cooler than in his room.

A nightbird sang its odd tune from the tree near the gate. Sometimes coyotes would follow the wash down from the parched foothills and look for dinner in the trailer park; that was probably what made the noise, though George didn't see any of the familiar gray shapes.

He turned to the right, would do a little perimeter walk around their trailer, make sure. There were footsteps behind him. His body tensed.

"I couldn't stay away—I had to see you," Jimbo whispered.

■ ■ ■

They could afford to stay at any hotel in the desert, though Jimbo was afraid of the looks and the questions they'd get if two young guys checked into a swank and straight golf resort at three thirty A.M. together with no luggage, no clubs, paying cash.

So they went to the Bluebird Motel, which was too close to Interstate 10 in Beaumont, so close in fact that George again lay awake in bed, starting at each new groan from a semi trailer trying to slow down as it slid into the Coachella Valley. The difference was that now Jimbo's arm lay draped across his belly—an improvement, for sure, over the Gomez trailer.

He flicked the sweat out from behind his ears, left over from the sexual exertion of the previous hour. Jimbo had no trouble sleeping like a baby. George shouldn't either, yet he lay awake.

He'd turned the phone off, but the screen lit up; someone was calling. At four in the morning.

Caller ID was blocked. George gingerly moved Jimbo's arm and swung his legs over the side of the bed. He took the phone and went onto the balcony.

"Hello?" Barely a whisper; he didn't want to wake Jimbo.

There was no voice on the other end, a tiny bit of static, something that sounded like a bell, perhaps, an uneven, random ringing.

Now, maybe it was his imagination or there really was a sharp intake of breath he could hear, one that he'd know anywhere. But still no voice.

"Connor? That you, right?"

He was sure he heard the man sigh. Above George, in the moonlight, the summit of Mount San Jacinto glistened with the last melting remnants of the previous winter's snow.

"So you have your money now, that's right, baby, but it's not as much as you thought?"

Heavier breathing; that ringing, now it sounded like a buoy—he was on the water somewhere.

"Because—I had to take my share. But I left the rest for you—for you and for Mrs. Greco."

George glanced back into the room, where Jimbo was asleep and waiting for him. The Marine slept fitfully, rolling over, sweeping his arm over the sheets where George should be.

"Because you would have cheated me and I could not let that happen," George said. "You are at the beach, Connor?"

Again he heard those bells—and finally, Connor's voice: "Jesus fucking Christ."

George slid the balcony door back open and stepped inside. "*Hasta,*" he whispered, disconnecting the call. He powered the phone off and got back into bed with Jimbo.

12

The new house wasn't in the best part of Cathedral City, which meant only that it was farther out into the desert and it took longer to get pizza for the boys.

There were advantages, however. Dead-end street, good new ranch construction in trendy shades of jade, foreclosure now vacant for over a year, and the seller didn't blink at a cash sale.

George could give this to Alma Gomez, literally—but it was for the boys, for Chuy and Jesse. They would grow up having it better, thanks to big brother. There was even a small pool in the back, room for a patio. Being able to provide, even with stolen property, made George proud and happy.

Jimbo loaded up the trunk of the new car—Mercedes, yes; new, well, new to them, anyway—with their bags, the combined wardrobes, which, admittedly, was not all that much.

"When will you be back?" Alma asked, standing on the walk, queen of her own little house, appearing taller than usual in her fresh, mall-bought pumps.

George knew the answer she hoped for was *never.* "Who knows, Mama?"

Jimbo had to rearrange the bags several times before he could get the trunk closed. "We took everything, even those *maricones* things you don't like."

Jimbo laughed. She didn't like him; George realized Alma was actually more afraid of this big white man from the American military than she was dismayed by the relationship he had with her oldest son. For his part, Jimbo had thrown twin Timbo under the bus, as they said *en inglés*, though George wished it was literal. Jim McLaughlin would be discharged in less than a month; he had his whole life ahead of him.

The two younger boys ran around the side of the house in their wet swimming trunks, orange and green water rifles dripping on the hot pavement. Afraid of a dousing, Alma covered her face and new hairdo, backing up the walkway to the front door.

George hugged the boys tight, Jesse with his left arm, Chuy with his right; though he would be close in Los Angeles, he would miss them and was wary of their mother's influence. He hadn't given her all the money he was planning on, not yet—so George Gomes would always retain influence over his brothers.

"Don't forget me," he said, and they laughed.

He watched them in the side mirror as Jimbo drove away, on their journey to west to L.A., the end of the road. George had this feeling, like other times earlier in his life, that this was the direction he should go. He didn't know what they'd find there, but it was a big enough place to ensure he could hide from both Connor and the Grecos if any of them got the stupid idea to come looking.

■ ■ ■

Kaya Belardo didn't like what she saw in the mirror, as she'd gained about eight pounds in the short weeks since Jacy had died. Makeup helped, and she'd taken her break partly to put on more but also because *they* were coming to the casino today and she was nervous.

She wasn't supposed to use the casino ladies' room, but because of her connection to Andreas, no other employees were going to say much of anything. It was a welcome sanctuary. She was teary less often, though she still cried a few times per shift when she'd remember a little something about Jacy, and the old ache would rise again like a volcano.

She dabbed at her dark eyes with one of their Egyptian hand towels branded with the Montana Grande logo. It was impossible to escape this! But why shouldn't she use one? It was the same family business that ultimately cheated her out of a future.

Since the tram "accident," Kaya had walked the res, usually to the places where she and Jacy had gone to tryst. Looking for him, or looking for a sign, anything that might tell her he was OK or that would give her a way forward or, better, a way out.

She guessed it was possible after all that those gray shrikes alighting on the res fence posts were his spirit guides; at least she felt less lonely when she saw them on her walks. She swore—to herself, anyway, if not to her relatives—that their message was to turn Andreas Alvarado in, even if doing so would destroy the casino.

But "they" always say anyone is replaceable. So, too, with him, she supposed.

She took out her eyeliner for a touch-up. Somebody would take pictures; she should look her best. Inside her purple blazer pocket, her phone made that little cricket noise, indicating a new text.

It was the guy from Indian Affairs. He said they were out front; it was just an FYI for her; he would not look her way if he saw her or otherwise acknowledge her. Her whistle-blower secret would be safe.

Because it was his fault, that Andreas. Jacy never would have become involved with the Grecos or their misguided alliance if Andreas—who all the native boys looked up to—hadn't suggested it, hadn't pushed it on him.

Now he'd pay.

Kaya heard voices raised before she even opened the ladies' room door. Male, all angry, everyone—well, everyone from the tribe. She exited the bathroom to the backs of patrons, the tourists cleared up away from the slot banks, the bells and electronic tunes oddly continuing despite the lack of players.

When Andreas finally appeared, flanked by two Native American agents, he wore his best poker face, total lack of expression. He held his head high, though she couldn't know for sure where he was looking because he also wore his sunglasses.

His anger would be something she'd need to navigate, but that would be down the road; that would not be something she had to do today. Today she would enjoy this spectacle of her own making.

It wouldn't bring Jacy back. But it was a start.

■ ■ ■

One of the half-truths Vi Gamble always told herself was that she had come up from hardy pioneer stock. The kind of people who could make things happen in the face of adversity, feathers not easily ruffled. She held on to that story of the family moving west during the Depression, held alive chiefly through inspiring fantasies encouraged by a collection of old black-and-white photos.

Which she was putting away into a box, to be added to the stack of boxes lined up in her front room, waiting for movers who would come eventually. Vi didn't even know for sure if the people in these photos were indeed her relatives, though years of belief told her they were. The message was always the same: We endure; we move on.

Turned out the cops had been unable to solve Locker's killing. There was no hard evidence against Vi, and she hadn't cracked, not even one tiny bit. The local detectives were more interested in getting back to their war on drugs. Besides, there were always burglaries and robberies along that stretch of Twentynine Palms Highway. Locker Hurst was just one unlucky guy.

She buried him in the cemetery overlooking a valley in Joshua Tree National Park. He'd always loved that place. It was just Vi and the minister at the grave. Duane still hadn't come back and Connor was now also MIA—instinctively, she knew these were connected but hadn't gotten to the bottom of it. But she would.

In the interim, there were the other things to attend to, the financial things. Meaning: She would accept the fact she was a failed drug dealer.

She would downsize, pull back, retrench. Even now that nice Korean real estate lady Marilyn Jeong—whose card she found before she left Locker on the floor of that garage—was pulling up into the driveway to pound a "For Sale" sign into the hard high-desert sand.

They did it together, right there on Anaconda Lane, Vi finding a hammer and spade. "Violet, you are going to make out like a bandit!" Marilyn said. "Morongo really is the *new* Palm Springs; you'll see."

■ ■ ■

Pilar Galindez Greco didn't like the massive molded-plastic boot on her foot, yet oddly she felt lighter. The boot, one of the visible casualties of her confrontation with Connor Hurst at the shipping office, wouldn't come off for another week.

It wasn't exactly fashion forward, but the symbolism was definitely freedom. Specifically—freedom from Sy Greco. Finally, putting her big foot down! At least, that's what she hoped people thought.

He'd left a cryptic message with Daniel that he "had to get out of town for a few days," but he hadn't been back and he certainly hadn't called her. It was over. Holding your spouse at gunpoint and then locking him in a closet didn't portend much of a reconciliation.

If anything bothered her, it was that annoying small-town newspaper and its reporter Ted Ligett, who had developed a surprising tenacity. She smiled to herself, thinking of whack-a-mole, where you got rid of one pest, then another popped up. This Ted had buried himself in Nancy Argento's files and had lots of questions.

That's the way they'd stay—just questions. No trace of her had been found, which, of course, made Pilar nervous. The pain pills for her ankle helped relieve some of that uncertainty. With each passing day the tiny, overworked Palm Springs cop shop would get preoccupied with whatever emergency thundered from their scanners. She hoped they'd forget Nancy soon enough.

Pilar had to do what she did. She kept reminding herself that it was not she who killed the reporter; it was that foolish *alte kaker* who didn't even bother to stop when he mowed her down. Sometimes remembering that helped. Not always.

She stood outside the Greco & Greco office on Palm Canyon as her workers Paco, Dante and Rodney maneuvered the former "Greco & Greco" sign off its mooring over the doorway. On the gravel strip next to the street waited the sign for her new venture, "Pilar Greco Real Estate" in bloodred letters, which she'd always heard was a good choice.

■ ■ ■

Connor wishes he had something stronger than that Tooheys New beer to keep him company in the Sydney night, that beer he's just thrown into the harbor's black water. Whiskey would be good. It's simple to buy one; the bar is open and that's what he'll do. After hanging up with George Gomes, he sure needs something.

He could've suspected him; it might have crossed Connor's mind once or twice to watch George carefully. He didn't, and now it is his problem. Even so, he has money—a lot of it, enough for a couple of years here in Oz, or wherever he wants—as long as he works it out right, as long as he's careful.

Funny how different these Sydney landmarks look in real life: the famous opera house, smaller, dirtier; the Harbour Bridge, not as big as he thought it would be. You can climb to the top; he thinks he sees a group preparing to do precisely that, perhaps for a dawn ascent. Connor shudders at the thought. The tram fall was too recent; his shoulder and his ankle still ache; the worst of it is at night.

Taking his cue from the Pilar Greco playbook, he'd sent the cash to himself in a number of small packages—books, he told the shipper, gifts for friends in New South Wales—and so far all had made it through. A lot of money, but still the totals are so far off what they should have been. The worst part is not that he doesn't have all of it—it's that George sucker punched him.

He rises from the waterside bench for the trip back to the bar. In front of him on the walkway are a young man and young woman, what you think of when you envision Australia: tan, blond, but not too much of either, extremely fit but without that mean tautness you find in California. A bonus is that she wears what must be 5 inch block heels on a platform of deep green leather.

Connor Hurst could definitely have a couple of beautiful years here.

Isn't that why you took the money to begin with? It wasn't to live a life free of Sy and Pilar Greco or Vi and Locker, or anyone else. It was to purchase this freedom. Sydney Harbour under the Southern Cross is apparently what that looks like, at least tonight.

And it's probable George Gomes, or Jorge Gomez, is a lot more like him than Connor wants to admit. In the end, he doesn't think it's his mother Alma's influence any more than Violet Gamble's conduct swayed Connor—the primal response for both men has always been to run in the exact opposite direction.

How odd it is he can so easily conjure up that fragrance of salvia, that reminder of old Mexico and young George, which he never gave much thought to when they were together. For one brief moment, he closes his eyes, and Connor is back in that empty mansion in Palm Springs, holding George tight against his chest.

www.ingramcontent.com/pod-product-compliance
Lightning Source LLC
Chambersburg PA
CBHW021102130626
46554CB00002B/498